D0260230

THE LIGHTNING CATCHER

CLARE WEZE

BLOOMSBURY
CHILDREN'S BOOKS
LONDON   OXFORD   NEW YORK   NEW DELHI   SYDNEY

BLOOMSBURY CHILDREN'S BOOKS
Bloomsbury Publishing Plc
50 Bedford Square, London WC1B 3DP, UK
29 Earlsfort Terrace, Dublin 2, Ireland

BLOOMSBURY, BLOOMSBURY CHILDREN'S BOOKS and the Diana logo
are trademarks of Bloomsbury Publishing Plc

First published in Great Britain in 2021 by Bloomsbury Publishing Plc

A catalogue record for this book is available from the British Library

ISBN: PB: 978-1-5266-2217-4; eBook: 978-1-5266-2218-1

2 4 6 8 10 9 7 5 3 1

Typeset by RefineCatch Limited, Bungay, Suffolk

Printed and bound in Great Britain by CPI Group (UK) Ltd, Croydon CR0 4YY

MIX
Paper from
responsible sources
FSC® C020471

To find out more about our authors and books visit www.bloomsbury.com
and sign up for our newsletters

For Rufus Weze and Orianu Weze

1

Moth Man

<u>*17th July*</u>

I'm not sure how you're meant to start journals, but here goes: We moved to Folding Ford in April and now it's July, and maybe it's because we're new here, but to me it's completely obvious that this village is cracked. Today the weirdness got major, which is why I'm going to start writing it all down. If something happens to me, everyone will know the facts, because of this journal.

Here's what happened today:

Only little kids believe in giants, but that's exactly what pounded down the hill, right at me. I was standing on the bridge at the edge of the village. It was dusk and I should have been home already.

He closed in fast, crazy white hair flying out, long string

of a body, big coat swinging with every step, like a cloak. And, OK, so up close I could see he wasn't a giant, but he *was* a ginormously tall man with a creepy face from a nightmare … and butterflies flapping around his shoulders.

The road was empty, the houses quiet and still.

Tried not to stare, but he was too tall, the butterflies were just too strange, and his snarly mouth and angry, darting eyes made him look ready to spring at anyone for any reason. I pretended something had got stuck in the front tyre of my bike, but my eyes were glued.

He scanned my face, a split-second glare that sent chills pulsing down my spine, chills that didn't stop, not even when he marched past me and away. And those weren't butterflies. They were brown, thick-bodied moths. And each one was tied to the man's wrists by a tiny thread.

He was taking them for a walk.

The giant with the moths is just the latest in a whole load of very strange things. Just in case anyone finds this notebook when I'm dead, here's a list of all the weird stuff that's happened since we moved here:

1. *A frozen puddle all by itself on a hot day in June. (Mum thought someone had emptied out their ice box on the pavement, but that was partly my fault. I shouldn't have prodded it before showing her.)*

2. *Thick frost on one branch of one tree near the primary school. Brilliant white, totally arctic and completely impressive (especially for June).*
3. *A whirlwind in one of Dad's beaten-up buckets, bubbling the water into demented spirals, and no wind anywhere else. (A salty smell came off it.)*
4. *A type of cloud I haven't seen in any other place. It's like a stack of pancakes with gaps in between.*
5. *My new best friend Sam's trainers iced up right in front of his eyes. He's been helping me look for clues ever since.*

All those weather freak-outs have *got* to be connected, so Sam and I are on high alert for clues about this weird over-load. My new Moth Man discovery is completely different, but he's linked – I'm sure of it. Sam and I will figure it all out and maybe get famous from it, and then this journal will be the official record of how we solve the mystery of Folding Ford.

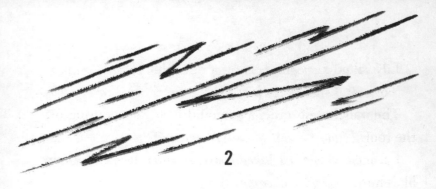

2

Fight! Fight!

<u>22nd July</u>

A massive day for the investigation! Discovered a HUGE amount of stunning new knowledge. Mum dragged us to a pointless jumble sale in the stupid village hall, and that's how it started, because guess what? The Moth Man was there.

As soon as he walked in, the entire room went quiet. Everyone turned to stare. The same mad hair streamed down his back. The same coat flapped behind like a giant bat had got loose. But no moths.

I grabbed my sister. 'Hey, Lily,' I whispered. 'Who *is* that?'

'How should I know? But whoa – he is so completely gigantic. Imagine how long his innards must be.'

'Remember the man with the moths I told you about?' I pointed at the Moth Man. '*Him!*'

Lily rolled her eyes. 'Give it a rest, Alfie.'

'For real. I swear.'

The hall was so quiet you could hear rain pouring off the roof.

I leaned closer to Lily. 'Look at their faces. Nobody likes him.'

'That lady does,' Lily said.

The Moth Man was rummaging through a stall full of electrical junk run by an old black lady – the only black person other than Dad that I've seen since we moved here – with silver beads threaded through her hair and a walking stick. He poked about impatiently, picking up an electrical extension cable without looking at her, even though she was talking nicely to him and smiling her head off.

The jumblers started to murmur again, softly, an up-and-down tune full of questions. Loads of eyes watched him hand money over, and he was every type of awkward a human can be. Kind of cross, but embarrassed, and also maybe in a massive sulk, like he hated the whole world. And he still gave me shivers.

'Ugh – looks like he's getting ready for something deadly. Someone so creepy shouldn't be buying that much cabling,' Lily said, like she was an expert.

'Look at his coat,' I said. 'Looks like it's made of skin.'

The Moth Man was on the move. This time, I had to

follow. He's the best clue I've seen since we moved here: a man who takes moths for a walk on a lead and turns a whole room silent. He *must* be something to do with the weirdness of this village.

'What are you doing?' Lily said, but I ignored her.

The Moth Man's coat still dripped. His hair looked like a dog's fur just before it shakes off the rain, and people made a big gap to let him pass.

I was brave. I got *sooo* close. Could have reached out and touched. The coat wasn't skin after all, but some oily fabric I've never seen before, and it smelt of horsey sawdust. He reminded me of a whopping, untrustworthy spider, and I got all jumpy again. I quite like spiders, but that feeling doesn't seem right for a human.

Mum blocked me. 'Where do you think you're going?'

'Just—'

'Oh no you don't. Mind your own business.' She gave me the stare of destruction.

The Moth Man was stomping off on heavy boots that would probably have liked to kick a few legs on the way out. Slipping away. Soon there was no sign of anyone towering and battishly cloaked.

'Can we just go, then? Home? This is for old people.'

'Nope. We're here to stay, and it won't kill you. We're still the new ones round here. We have to show our faces.'

'As if anyone's even noticed us—'

'Don't argue with me, Alfie Bradley. Stay where I can see you. Don't break anything – in fact, don't *touch* anything. And don't forget to say "please" and "thank you".'

Lily popped up behind her. 'Yeah, Alfie, zero touching. Got it?'

What was I supposed to do? I toured the hall, but there was nothing cool in the entire room, just stinky clothes piled on tables like junk mountains. Bo*ring* – until Lily came up to me, giggling behind her hand.

'There's a full-on shouty-crackers fight in the kitchen,' she said, signalling me to follow. It didn't look like a Lily wind-up, and Mum was bending over a stall.

'They're arguing about your giant,' Lily said. 'He rescues weird animals from abroad and they keep escaping and Mr Fuming says it's dangerous and Mrs Cranky says it isn't.'

'Who? *Who?*'

She took me to a tiny corridor between the main hall and the kitchen. The kitchen door wasn't completely closed, and through the gap we could see the old lady from the electrical-junk stall leaning against the counter. She was the one rowing, and she was doing it with an old man I hadn't seen before, and because the noise from the main hall was like a million murmuring penguins, we were the only ones listening.

This new old man was red in the face and bulgy in the neck, with bristly white side-hair sticking up round the edges of his bald head like a brush. Lily was right – they were having a fantastic blow-up, shouting over each other like we're not supposed to at school. All I understood was, *Don't ever invite him to a parish event again!* (The old man spat that.) And, *Don't you dare tell me who I can and can't invite!* (The old lady yelled this.) And then they stopped and glared at each other.

'You missed the best bits,' Lily said. 'She kept telling him to get knotted.' She put her earbuds back in and skipped away.

I got into perfect secret-listening position, like a detective: body hidden in a corner, head angled round. See without being seen.

The old man started up again. 'This village hasn't been the same since that miscreant came back.'

The lady rapped her fingers along the counter and gave him an impressively fatal scowly look.

'As head of the parish council, I have a duty to police his mess and botching.' His voice was croaky, and deep, like a walrus. 'We've had enough of his marauding animals – they're always escaping. That monstrous bird on the allotments last summer – the damage it did! Spiteful-looking creature. Vermin! Folding Ford is no place for zoo rejects.'

Then he aced it. 'All the children are afraid of him

and it's not the sort of thing we want in this village. Experimental animal breeding, warped hybrids – it's not right. Hellish goings-on at that house.'

The lady made a superb lip-puckered face at him and said, 'Ash House is an animal *sanctuary*, not a—'

'Don't play the innocent,' he snapped. 'We've both seen what's escaped from there. A stampede of giant mutant guinea pigs last spring! Ash House is a charnel house!'

The lady looked at the ceiling and groaned. Whatever a charnel house is, she doesn't like them.

Ash House. The last house in the village. I knew it straight away – we drove past when we were still exploring new places to live, just before we moved here. It's big, white, and stands on its own with huge fir trees in the garden. Those trees are the best ever. They sway in the wind, leaning together like they're whispering.

More shouting. More muddle. I couldn't see what was so bad about bringing things into the country from abroad and making wind traps and messing about with stuff and inventing junk – sounded cool to me – but the old man thought it was bad, bad, *baaad*.

'… you name it, he's dragged it back with him like a bagful of Beelzebub's beetles.' He stopped to snigger at his own cleverness, then went on even more spittingly than before. 'Greasy, poisonous things – all those spitting frogs.

And now he's tampering with the electricity supply! All those contraptions of his should be smashed and stopped. Every last one of them.'

'Don't be ridiculous!' the lady said. 'Nathaniel Clemm is harmless. You're the one who needs stopping.'

So the Moth Man was called Nathaniel Clemm.

'Harmless? Spinal cords lying around the place, and you call that harmless?'

Spinal cords!

'Well,' the lady said, 'vultures have to eat.'

'Vultures!'

'Just one vulture,' she said, drumming her fingers again. Her nails flashed silver, like Christmas decorations. 'And she didn't stay long – he was just sheltering her between zoos. He's a conservationist, not a butcher. You want to round up anyone who's not the same as you, don't you? You can't stand people who are different.'

With a ridiculous walrus-like '*Harrumph!*' the old man turned his back on the lady and stomped out of a side door. The lady looked like she might come my way, so I sneaked back into the main hall and blended in like a total spy. The investigation was going better than I could possibly have hoped, but what was the next step?

Suddenly it was obvious: I'd go and look at this spooky old charnel house myself.

Thought I'd got past Mum easy. She was trying to make Lily eat a cupcake, which is just about impossible because Lily hardly eats anything since she got bullied super badly when she moved up into Year Eight last year. (That's why we had to move here, to get Lily a brand-new life.) Anyway, Lily and Mum were in a cupcake standoff, but Mum must have clocked me, and just as I reached the door, she struck.

'Where do you think you're off to now?'

Never even knew she *could* creep up on people.

'Need fresh air,' I said. Then a brainwave happened. 'And can I meet up with Sam? I've done nearly an hour here.' Sam would freak when I told him about Nathaniel Clemm and Ash House. We could recce the place together.

She looked at me suspiciously.

'It'll give me more exercise …'

Her mouth stretched into a straight line with dimples at each end, which meant I'd won but she still disapproved. 'Go on then. But you're going nowhere without this.' She pulled out my blue padded monstrosity of a coat from nowhere that made any sense.

'Not that puffy thing! It's hardly even raining now.'

'No coat, no go. You *will* need it, and you *will* take it.'

I grabbed the evil thing and cleared out.

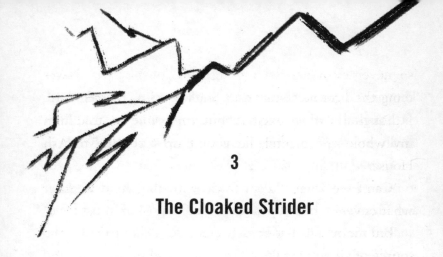

3

The Cloaked Strider

Persuading Sam to come with me was easy – at first. Went home for my bike, then texted, *Meet me at Eggshell Bench. Got intel!*

Sam: *What intel?*
Me: *Too long – tell you in person*

(That sounded professional. I'm getting good at this.)

Eggshell Bench sits at the top of stone steps on a steep grass banking, and you can hide there because it's always overgrown. It's one of our best places. The back of the bench curves over like a smooth plastic eggshell – like it got dropped on the way to a children's playground – and that's how it got its name.

By the time I'd biked there the stupid rain had stopped,

so never even needed my senseless puffer coat. I was tying the horrific thing to the saddle when Sam arrived. I thought he'd be excited, but even when I told him my whole entire intel, he wasn't up for going to Ash House.

'Can't see what it's got to do with the weird weather whatsoever.'

'But, Sam, this is our best clue yet. This might be the source of all Folding Ford's secrets,' I said majestically and watched him thinking. He's in the top set in all subjects at school, and sometimes you can hear his brain working. 'And it's a charnel house.'

'A *what*?'

'Yeah, sounds awful. Needs looking up.'

Sam got it done before I'd taken my next breath and said, 'It's a house full of bodies or bones, or *death*!'

'Whoa. See?'

'Still don't fancy it,' he said. He stared at his front bike wheel, scraping it with the toe of his trainer.

My belly felt like beetles were crawling in it and I went hot all over. 'Why not?'

'He's *well* scary. We call him the Cloaked Strider, because he walks round in that big long coat like a total randomer. Roan used to have nightmares about him.'

Roan is Sam's little brother. 'So the giant on Beggar's

Hill with all those moths – that was the Cloaked Strider?' I said. 'You never told me.'

'You didn't mention any cloak. You were all about a giant with moths on threads – which is impossible, actually. Moths shed scales if you even pretend to touch them.' Sam lives on a farm; he knows the most amazing stuff about any animal. 'If you tried to tie threads on moths, they'd slither away leaving you totally scaled up.'

'Which doesn't stop it from being true that day. I know what I saw.'

He shook his head at me, slowly. 'Anyway, he's *properly* weird. Dodge Cooper's brother says he comes out at night like a bat, and never sleeps. I'm not going near him.'

'But if we just do a little spy work from the road,' I said, rolling my bike down the steps and hoping he'd follow. 'It'll be fine. Come on – he won't even know.'

'There was no Cloaked Strider when my trainers iced up,' Sam said. 'The cold was just suddenly there and I stepped right into it. I'd have seen him.'

'That old guy made it sound like he does things from a distance. We might be able to see his long-range weather-warper machines through the hedge.'

Sam's face went very still and he scanned the village below us, like he was connecting things in his head. Like bits of curiosity were sprouting in his brain. I could almost hear them glooping together.

'We totally need to find out if that old guy's on to something.' I'd reached the road by now. 'Need to find out what a *miscreant* is. Sounds like something worth seeing – probably a deformed monkey, or something.'

'Nope. Not what it means. A miscreant is a kind of villain.'

'Only you would know that,' I said, but he pretended he hadn't heard and let a long sigh bubble out through pressed-together duck lips.

'A villain!' I said. 'Even better. Even more likely to be up to weather-warping business … especially if he's breeding dodgy animal mixtures. Weird goes with weird. Maybe he's planning to whip up a massive storm of mutant clouds that can push through doors and windows and suffocate everyone. Maybe he's lacing them with chemicals. And there are *spinal cords* lying around up there and everything!'

'Spinal cords? Where? How?'

I shrugged. 'Could be anywhere.'

Sam rolled his bike chain forward and back. It didn't need any fiddling, so I knew his brain was chewing through things. Then he bombed to the bottom step, did an excellent wheelie and skidded on to the road.

'Right,' he said. 'Are we going or not?'

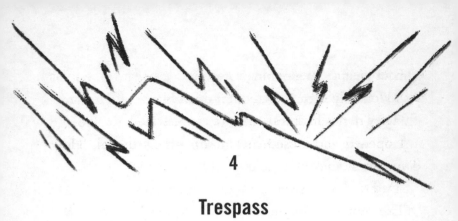

4

Trespass

Soon we were out on Halfway Lane, where the sky is always enormous. Hardly any traffic goes through that way, so we rode side by side.

Sam braked. 'There it is.'

Ash House. Big. White. On its own behind tall hedges with fields on every side and a jumble of barns at the bottom of its big long garden. There aren't any other houses at this end of the lane, so it stands lonely. That's all. Doesn't sound like enough to make it creepy, but it is.

'Where's he keep the animals?' I asked.

'Mostly at the back in those barns,' Sam said. 'It goes way back.'

'Come on, we need to get closer.' Couldn't stop thinking about those spinal cords, but I had to be cool. 'Look at the wind. It's only in the fir trees.'

Four gigantic trees swayed and strained near the side of Ash House, like guard dogs that might snap.

'They're not fir trees – they're cypresses.'

I opened and closed my mouth – he's unreal. 'How d'you know that?'

'Dad told me. We've got one.'

The noise went high and then low as the wind climbed and fell like a bunch of witches moaning. Then it came closer and whined through the top of the hedge, high and screechy, like someone had set it free. Then silence.

'Ha!' I said. 'This place is creep city. How can the wind come from nowhere so fast? Maybe he's got a weather machine.'

'If there's even any such thing …' Sam's eyebrows went frowny and surprised. 'Look at that.'

A bunch of seagulls had been picking over the soil in the field next to the Strider's trees. I'd noticed them out of the corner of my eye – bending their heads to the ground, pecking at things – but now every single seagull head was upright and looking around.

'See that?' Sam said. 'Like it was a plan.'

The back of my neck tingled. 'What've they heard?'

All together, the seagulls took one step towards the trees and lifted their heads to the sky. They took another step, and bowed their heads down low, shaking their tail feathers, all still heading for one tree.

I felt the hairs at the back of my neck rising. But then the seagulls took off. They flew towards that one tree, then glided around in the air above it, easily, as if they were surfing on something invisible that was pouring from it.

My breath came out in a squeak. 'Yo. Time to ride air currents.'

The wind stopped and the branches dropped, like someone big had let them go.

And then the seagulls flew away in different directions, leaving us staring at nothing but empty treetops.

We biked up to the main gateway and looked across the front garden at the house. My heart still thudded from the seagulls, but there was no car, no sign of anyone home. Dark windows with nothing moving behind them. Dirty grey cracks running down the white walls like lightning streaks. A plant had grown up as far as the roof, then died. Brown strings of it hung like a mouldy beard.

I inched towards the gateway. Sam didn't move.

'Hey, come on,' I said. 'I know you've heard freaky stories, but we won't find out anything till we investigate. All that Cloaked Strider junk might be a trick. He keeps everyone out – he gets to do whatever he's doing in secret.'

That didn't explain the seagulls. Sam looked like he was thinking that exact thought.

I took a deep breath, said, 'Yay, nobody in!' then ditched my bike and did football-celebration moves in the gateway.

'Stop it, twit,' Sam snapped.

'What's wrong? There's nobody to see us. Weather machines and weird beasts, remember? Just a quick look in case we can see something working.'

Sam stayed on his saddle while I peered round the gate. He looked completely jumpy and picked at his fingernails, as if he couldn't quite believe I'd talked him into coming.

Then something bounced out of the long grass and my heart nearly left my chest. My brain took a moment to work it out. Was *that* really a cat? It had *no hair*.

Its pink skin was wrinkled in some places, smooth in others. Its ears were like bat's ears – far too much of their knobbly insides were showing – and it bounded up to us like we were the most important things it had seen all day.

I did nothing but point at it for seconds, speechless. Then I said, 'See? Proof! Weird stuff's going off here for sure. Looks like a cross between a cat, a kangaroo and a bat.'

Sam blinked at it. He looked a bit sick. 'You *can* get bald cats, but that's pretty weird. It looks like pig skin. Drastic wrinkles.'

The cat walked off, looking over its shoulder at us and meowing.

'It's trying to tell us something,' I said.

'Have you lost it, or what? It might be a freak, but it's still only a stupid cat.'

I snorted. '*Whaaat?* Erm – that is not just a cat. Look at it, will you!'

'OK – a stupid bald cat. No need to flip out on me.'

'*No*, it's trying to *show* us something. It wants us to follow. It's obvious.'

'Only if you're cat-crazed.'

'Perhaps it's got kittens. Stuck somewhere.' I untied my coat, stuffed it into the hedge and took a step inside the gates.

'What are you doing? Come back, you utter—'

'Just wanna see what she's trying to tell us,' I said. 'The man's out – he won't even know.'

'You can't! You're not allowed in people's gardens, not round here. Especially not his house!'

'Well *you* don't have to. Stay there. Keep watch. I'm not a vandalist.'

'You melter! No!'

But I was already inside.

5

Weird Goes with Weird

In the gateway, Sam watched me, eyes wide, hands gripping his handlebars, one foot up on a pedal, ready to go.

The cat sat next to a wrecked piece of wire near the trees at the side of the house, twitching its tail. Waiting for me.

The rest of the garden stretched out behind the house, endless, as big as a field, long grass rippling like a sea. My heart danced – there was room for *anything* in there. Bits of metal poked up everywhere like a ruined city.

Up in the branches, wire blended into the leaves and twigs, almost perfectly. Mr Clemm must have strung it there, masses of it. Not sure, but it looked like telephone wire. Are people even allowed to mess with telephone wire?

A broken rowing-machine-type thing crouched horribly in the long grass near the cat. My heart thumped and my face went hot, but – oddly – my legs were freezing. I looked back for Sam but couldn't see him now: I'd come too far.

The cat plunged into a tangle of plants under the trees, scattering midges like splatters of paint, and I followed, smooth as an eel, treading sideways to squash a mat of weeds to walk on. Soon I was beneath the first massive tree.

The second one had branches that swept down to the ground like a living tent, and that's where the cat went. I buried my face in the waving tips, breathing in the woody, dusty pine smell and waiting, listening, like Dad says I should. It's better than crashing around.

The cat curled herself between the thick tree roots and fixed her weird blue eyes on mine. The tree-tent gave her a greenish tinge. Then she did a quick wash: chest, stomach creases and leg creases. It must be like wearing a baggy suit. (Wow. I haven't got the words for how amazing this cat is. No whiskers or even eyelashes.)

Then *crackle*, *snap*, *patter* – she skittered off sideways into an open patch of ground. I followed, and that's when I saw the box.

The box is today's *outstanding* piece of evidence.

6

The Prisoner

The box was in a clearing. Mr Clemm must have sunk it into the ground near his trees and let everything grow around it. Made of metal and as long as me, it didn't make any sense. And yes, I did think *coffin*.

When I took a step closer, my heart nearly stopped – everything I'd thought was a leaf or a twig twitched into life. *Moths*. Dozens of them, quivering on every millimetre of the box. As I watched, still as a statue, they calmed down until their wings were just opening and closing slowly. These were some of the Moth Man's moths, for sure. Might they let me take them for a walk?

And was this a moth trap?

Seconds went by. Minutes, probably. I crouched down and reached for the box. I did it slowly, but it was too much. They fluttered away in every direction.

The box's lid was made of blue glass. Shiny silver wires ran along the sides and over the top, like something scientific was going on. Sweat beads prickled all over my face, but I touched the lid. It was still wet from the rain and *so* smooth. Close up, the box smelt of tar.

A beetle trundled past my foot, and that's when I noticed how cold everything was going. In seconds, it was freezing, like someone had emptied a bagful of ice-cold air over my head. One of the laces on my trainers totally iced up.

I stood and took a step back – and the cold vanished. Feeling all electrified with nerves, I squatted again and felt around the air. A perfect tall square of sharp coldness started about a metre above the box and ended right on one side of the lid. The air next to it was as warm as anything.

The cat wound herself round my legs again and again; I'd almost forgotten about her. Then, all quivery and happy, she jumped on to the box and pawed over twigs and dead ivy as neat and light as a dancer, as if tracing her paws over steps drawn out beforehand. This was obviously one of her favourite places. When she came to the cold part, she stopped. Her skin rippled and twitched.

Then, like she'd wound around my legs, the cat rubbed herself against part of the lid of the thing and something came loose. She pushed her head against the wires, as if the box itself was going to feed her. And then the thing that was always going to happen happened: the stupid cat butted the loose part off completely.

It made a heavy thud on the undergrowth, louder than you'd believe possible from the size of it, and the cat jumped off, all scared, as if she hadn't even done anything.

I poked the loose part with my toe – it was a metal bar – and then I left it there. Didn't know what else to do. Couldn't make sense of where it fit or what it might be for—

A tiny noise came from the box.

A movement.

Something was inside. Something bigger than a moth.

My head and neck tingled. The thing inside moved again; something was definitely trapped. Could an animal have got into a moth trap somehow? The cat sat on a tree root, staring at me, calm now. Waiting.

I felt for the fastenings. *Really shouldn't ...*

But I couldn't leave an animal to suffer and maybe die. There were no fastenings. No ordinary ones, anyway. And nothing budged when I pulled a metal loop on the front edge. I bent down still further and squinted through a crack where the side joined the top. The body of a spider lay millimetres from my eye, squashed as flat as if it had been ironed.

Another tug on the corner of the lid and something loosened. Now each tug made a creaking, splintering noise.

A smell of rusty metal and damp and toadstools seeped out. I looked behind again, listening for footsteps, then pulled more gently. After a while, the lid opened a crack. It couldn't have been more than a centimetre, but in that tiny space everything changed.

The whole box buzzed. I jumped away, but not before a tiny stingy-burning feeling got me on the forehead. My hair rose in the air on its own. The whole box crackled, and for a microsecond, my teeth fizzed.

Something rushed past me, brushing my arm, prickling my skin.

Something *fast*. Faster than the wind.

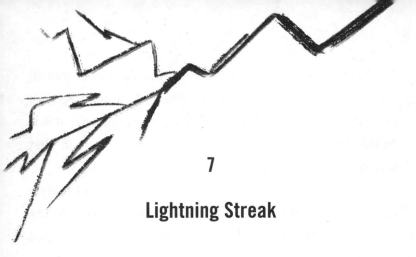

7

Lightning Streak

Whatever it was left a strange smell behind: hot metal, like warm coins held in your hand for too long. And the air felt tight and unbreathable.

My forehead still tingled where the thing had touched it. I pulled the lid again, and this time I got a tiny electric shock – like the ones you get from car door handles. But the lid opened properly at last, on a hinge. Inside, the box was empty, apart from a rubbery sheet at the bottom, a jumble of clips with coiled wires coming off them and something that looked like tinfoil. The walls were metal, with wooden rails halfway up. The wooden parts looked a bit burned. I leaned over to get a better view. A tiny, clear puddle of water glimmered on the sheet.

A clicking noise ticked on and off, like the gas fire in our old house after someone had switched it off.

Tick-tick click.

Too much spit in my mouth now. I closed the cage contraption and fastened everything back the way it had been, as fast as I could, shakily, with jelly fingers. Then I stood up and backed away from the box, looking all around – on the ground, in the air – but there was no sign of whatever had been inside. There was only the cat, still sitting and staring at me. I wiped an itch on my nose – a tingling itch – and looked down at my shaking hands.

The cat twisted her neck round and nibbled an itch on her back. A little breeze blew the long grass into her face. She finished dealing with the itch in three fast licks, then turned to stare at a space above my head. And at the same moment, I felt something again.

Electricity in the air.

Stronger this time, like when you stand next to a pylon. And even the ground felt different: the soles of my feet buzzed.

The cat put one ear back, but the rest of her body was fixed in stiff listening mode. She felt it too. I didn't like that. What did she know now? Her tongue licked out for no reason I could see, like she was tasting the air.

Then she turned to stare in the direction of the house and seemed to relax completely. A moment later came the sound of car tyres crunching over gravel, and the cat trotted away happily, heading for the house.

The buzzing was gone. But Nathaniel Clemm was back. My breathing went all shattered. Sweat sprouted from lots of places on top of my head all at once. A car door slammed. Footsteps crunched. I shot under the tree-tent, scattering a crowd of tiny flies, then crouched and listened and wished I hadn't come. How old was he? Could I outrun him?

I darted back to the path at the side of the house – hating the giveaway sound of stuff crushing under my feet – then realised something horrible: I was trapped. I'd have to wait for Mr Clemm to go into the house, otherwise he'd see me. But once he was inside, how could I get past those long windows without being seen? And where was Sam? Had he hidden my bike?

The silence was worse than the footsteps.

Then I realised – there *was* another way out of this garden. It was a hard way, but better than walking in front of the house. I headed further into the trees, wading through nettles too big to squash down. If I could climb the huge garden hedge and get into the field, I could run away without being seen. *If.*

You don't really climb *over* hedges. You climb through them, and it's very hard. They're a thousand times thicker than you think.

At the other side, just as I tore free from the thorns and branches – leaving bits of my jeans behind – Sam's text landed:

Sam: *Moved your bike to Eggshell Bench. Gone home*

Hadn't meant to make such a total wreck of the hedge. I'd stretched it, which shouldn't be possible, but you could definitely see gaps where I'd been.

Shot across the field and headed for the road, where I'd be safe and legal – but as I was climbing the final gate, a little electric shock vibrated through my hands and feet.

I thought that was it, but I'd taken about three steps on the tarmac when a whopping crack of thunder sounded behind me and I looked back. Ash House was under a massive black cloud. It hung low and lashed rain at the house like the roof was its target. Thunder crashed again. There was no lightning, but a warm wind blew down the lane straight into my face and spooked me. It smelt eggy and bitter. I started sprinting, but when I looked back, it was all over.

The cloud brightened then disintegrated. Halfway Lane went back to its full summer day, as if nothing had happened.

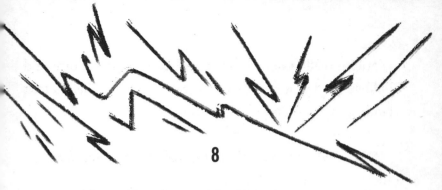

8

The Stupid Puffer Coat

<u>23rd July</u>

Sam's furious with me. 'I *only just* got away with both bikes before the Cloaked Strider came back,' he said on the phone last night. 'What if he'd caught us?'

'But he didn't.'

'Brainless, the whole idea,' he said. His voice was fast and cold and full of sharp edges.

Things improved when I told him all about the box. I tumbled the words into the phone before he could hang up.

'You let something *loose?*'

I fed him every single detail. I knew he'd get fired up. 'The opening it came out of was minuscule, Sam – I mean, it was a tiny crack. And yet something ultra weird came out. We need to find out what.'

'You're really not exaggerating about the speed of it?'

'Absolutely not. It was mega fast, like lightning. Come round tomorrow and I'll show you the box.'

'No way.'

'OK, well maybe we could just ride up and down outside the house and see if anything's visible—'

'Yeah, that's what you said last time and look what happened.'

'No crime in biking on the road. Think about it.'

After Sam, I wanted to tell someone else. Lily wouldn't have believed me in a trillion years, so I texted Dad. Can't wait to see what he thinks of my adventure. Obviously didn't mention the trespassing.

Dad's texted back to say he's too busy to text.

But the most brilliant, stupendous, incredible idea's just hit me: I'm going to email some of this actual journal to Dad, in Sweden. Just the best bits, I mean. The safe bits. Not the parts where I break rules and stuff. Those would singe his hands and set his teeth on fire and he'd ground me for a month. Look out, Mr Jerome Bradley.

Dad just phoned.

'That's a lot of material you've sent me, Alfie.'

'Well, you said it gets boring building river bridges ...'
I said.

'It can.'

'And your steel sometimes messes up when they pour it,
and you get headaches.'

'If people don't do what they've promised,' he said,
'ye-e-s ...'

'Right, well you'll never be bored now you've got this
journal to read. It's my official record. I'm going to solve—'

'Yes, cracking journal-keeping, Alfie!' he said, with too
much awesome in his voice. 'And a giant, too.'

'Not really an actual giant ...'

'Oh, OK. Yeah, sorry, I'll get deeper into it later.'

'And the weird creature I let loose?' I said. 'Have you
even read it properly?'

'Ah – did have to skim a little, but promise I'll make
time for it soon. Now, listen, Lily hasn't been in touch at
all. How does she seem to you?'

'Same,' I said. He's always asking me about Lily. I think
he's scared she'll start living in bed again. 'She's getting up,
she's going to school – mostly – and when she comes home,
she's annoying. Normal.'

'Really?'

Who wouldn't be OK if they went to Lily's school?
I'd be fabulous if I went to a tiny school in a special,

funky house for people who've been messed up by bullies. They get to do photography and film-making. There's no assembly, PE is usually swimming (every day! In a pool the temperature of bathwater, Lily says!), you don't have to go outside every break time, and they do tons of art and crafts. Dad doesn't get it. How could Lily fail to be OK?

Couldn't say any of that, so I just said: 'Genuinely,' and tried to steer him back to my magnificent discoveries. I was working up to asking him if he thought it was OK to release all trapped creatures – any trapped creature – even if you'd found them in someone's garden, when he said:

'You didn't say what happened with your coat.'

My COAT! My blasted coat … is still in the hedge!

At the exact moment I was thinking this, Sam came to the door with a pair of small binoculars around his neck. 'We can do an observation from the road,' he said. 'But that's definitely all.'

'Got to go,' I told Dad. 'Bye.'

'Emergency!' I yelled at Sam. 'My stupid puffer coat! Quick!'

Lily appeared on the front lawn and tried to stop us with a tragic speech about Mum not knowing where I was going, and that without permission it was impossible for me to leave, but I laughed in her face.

'Don't need it,' I said, and we started biking. 'I'll text her. Gotta go.'

'I'm in charge while Mum's at work.'

'No you're not. You *keep an eye*. That doesn't mean you're in charge.'

'Yes it *does*!' Lily screamed this at our disappearing backs.

We rode back to Ash House like two mad streaks of lightning, pumping the pedals, not caring how sweaty we got.

'It's not here,' I said, looking at the piece of hedge where my coat should have been. My knees felt very quivery.

The car wasn't there either. Ash House was deserted again.

Sam stomped around the piece of hedge, still looking, then gave up. 'So someone's got it. Tell me it hasn't got your name in it.'

I nodded. My mouth was dry and horrible.

He shook his head. 'I told you this whole idea was idiotic. So now there's solid proof that you were hanging around his house when this thing escaped. Nice one.'

The wind started up in the trees. A minute ago they were waving gently, like friends saying hello. Now they circled round and round, faster and faster.

'Look at that,' I said. 'And it isn't even windy anywhere else.'

Sam didn't say anything.

'Right,' I said, 'I'm showing you that box.'

Sam shook his head slowly. 'No, I'm not getting dragged into this trespassing craziness.' He made a big show of looking at the waving trees through his binoculars.

I said, 'You're too careful.'

'You're too sloppy!'

'I don't get you, Sam. You're the science ninja. There's all this sciency stuff going on in there – inventions and whizzing creatures – and what do you do? You disappear!'

'Of course I disappeared! It's because I'm NOT STUPID! You might not care if people think you're trash, but why would I want a loser's reputation? You don't seem bothered about that, but it's a real thing, and just you wait till it actually happens.'

'Hey, Sam, look around. You do know we're completely alone here, don't you? It's all OK. There's no need to liquidise yourself completely.' Although I did feel a bit sorry for him – his mum's much stricter than mine.

His mouth twitched a bit – almost a smile.

'We'll be really, *really* careful. You escaped last time like a total pro!'

'Huh – it was almost a disaster. He's got an old Bentley, so it made hardly any noise,' he said. 'Didn't hear it till nearly too late.'

I nodded. I don't know cars like Sam does. 'Hide the bikes in the hedge this time,' I said. 'We'll be experts. Gladiators. We'll be so slick …'

I scraped the tarmac with my trainer, holding my breath, pretending I wasn't really all squirmed up with hope.

Sam sighed. 'In, quick look, then out again,' he said, jabbing his thumb towards the garden and back to the road. 'Right?'

We found a gap, shoved our bikes away, then darted into the garden. Sam's eyes were as wide as fried eggs, but we were in. I couldn't believe he was actually doing it, and it felt fantastic.

We made for the trees. At the edge of Mr Clemm's broken path, the wind found us and blasted into our faces. A pile of tiny, delicate bones lay deep in the grass, all white and clean. Sam blinked at them, bending closer.

'Those weren't there before,' I told him, feeling excited in a shivery way. 'Watch out for nettles.'

'You can see where you went last time,' he said. 'You've squashed the weeds.'

He was right. A trail of squashed undergrowth led from the path to the biggest tree. I'd murdered my cover.

I started kicking up the nettles. 'Push them back to normal.'

'Too late – he's probably seen it by now. Come on.'

A carpet of moss covered the main path and, above it, the wires hung, slack and strange. When we found the box, Sam's eyes were everywhere at once: on the wires, over his shoulder, through the trees, back to the box.

'Did you actually get an actual electric shock?'

I nodded. 'My feet buzzed. Even my teeth fizzed.' I pointed to my forehead. 'Still tingling from where the creature brushed past.' This was only partly true. The feeling disappeared when I wasn't concentrating on it.

The wind above us sounded wispy now, like breath, as if it was caught on something.

I pulled the hinge open carefully, ready to spring away if anything moved. 'Look at these wires and this shiny sheeting. Some electrical gubbins, isn't it? And there was a little puddle of water here before. The cold spot was just here.' I showed him. 'This has to be connected to the weather stuff.'

Sam crouched. 'Weird. Might be an experiment.' He poked a finger into the spaghetti wires that spilt down the outside edges, lifting carefully.

'Hey, don't electrofry yourself to death!'

He ignored me and let the wires down gently. 'Copper wire. And look at these.' He pointed at some tinier wires in one corner. 'Thin as hairs.'

I whistled. Hadn't even noticed them.

'So something to do with electrical conductivity do-dahs,' he said. 'You got a little shock. You said there was crackling, so that must have been static.' He tapped the blue glass. 'Yep. This is a solar panel. He must be running something off the sunlight.' He squinted up into the tree and a gust of wind blew his hair upside down. 'Look. It's hidden in all these trees, but there's a bare place where the sun gets through quite well.'

I grinned. 'Knew your savvy would come in handy!'

Sam blushed. 'Yerp, well ... my auntie's got some on her roof. Exactly the same blue.'

Sam stood up and so did I. He looked down at the box. 'A bat could move quickly.'

'Nope. It was too fast.'

'Some kind of insect?'

I shook my head. 'It was more like a piece of wind.'

He laughed. 'Wind doesn't come in pieces. It's just moving air.'

'Well, this isn't just a cage – it looks too clever and complicated for that.'

Sam nodded. 'Yah, he must be feeding electricity into this for a reason.'

'Maybe it's a life-support system!'

Sam widened his eyes at me. 'Cool!' he said, nodding slowly. 'Of course.'

'For an electrical creature! I got two electric shocks, so that makes sense. An experiment that went wrong!'

Sam's eyes were wild. 'An electrical creature?'

'He must have bred it – you know, like people say.'

He grinned. 'That's just *ill*.'

'There are electric eels, aren't there?' I said.

'Yerp. So …?' (Sam never ever says the word 'yes'. Not unless he's spitting mad.)

'Maybe he got one and experimented on it. That old man said he mangles things. Maybe it's a mangled electric eel.'

'On dry land?' Sam said. 'Heh! Yah, Alfie, not one of your better ideas. There's no creature that's made of *only* electricity.' He frowned at me sceptically. 'Are you really sure you saw this thing?'

I remembered something else. 'After it escaped, the box clicked and ticked, like gas fires when you switch them off. Like metal contracting.'

'So something hot had been in there.' His eyes brightened. He opened his mouth to say more, but at that exact moment the wind stopped. It didn't die away; it stopped in mid-blow, like a gasp.

'That's exactly what happened last time,' I whispered.

He grabbed my arm. 'Quiet!'

We listened. Crows circled the rooftop, then flew off silently. It was so still, we could hear falling cypress needles click and flutter through the branches.

'No hair,' Sam breathed into my ear. I could tell his brain was whirling now or he'd have been too scared to make a noise. 'That cat kept climbing on the box, you said. And now it's got no hair. What if it was a normal cat and not a bald breed? What if all the electricity made the cat bald?'

I touched my hair, feeling suddenly horrible. 'Can electricity do that?'

'It might.'

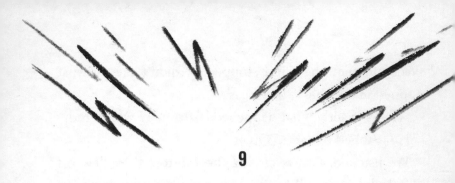

9

Stampede in the Mist

Then something squealed. Something huge. The noise came from behind the house, way back in the garden, maybe even as far down as the barns. A loud bleat, then a wheezy rattle, like a sheep being strangled.

We looked at each other and quickly scrambled back to the path.

'Woo!' I said. 'What sort of animal could even make that noise?'

'Best not to interfere. Come on – let's get out of here.'

He was right, but what if it was the super-fast creature? 'No – whatever it is might be stuck. *You* know that, farm boy.'

'Alfie, we can't get caught here – we need to leave *right now!*'

'Sorry – gotta find out,' I said, and raced towards the bleating.

I thought he'd leg it home, but – unbelievably – Sam followed and we plunged through the gloomy wilderness, using hands as well as feet to stop the weeds snarling us up. Old farm machinery stuck up here and there like giant tragic sculptures. Things we couldn't see made muffled scurrying noises, and for the first time, it felt like we were on our own somewhere strange and unpredictable, and perhaps this wasn't such a great idea.

The squealing and bleating got louder and more frantic.

Sam was a couple of steps behind me. 'Wait,' he said, 'is it coming towards us?'

I shook my head, totally baffled – the noise sounded like it was in front of us, behind us and even above – but then things got even more scrambled because something else was happening at the same time: MIST. It dropped down on us thickly, from nowhere, and we were already deep in an over-grown tangle. It took seconds for everything to disappear except our faces, which now looked like eerie deformed moons. Apart from that, we couldn't see a thing so had to stop.

Sam stuffed his binoculars in his pocket and said, 'No way.'

I shivered. Don't know why I'm calling it mist, because it was like somebody had dumped a full, soaking cloud on to Ash House and all its grounds. After a few seconds, we could see a tiny bit more: the mist was moving. It travelled across the garden in one thick, chilling mass, making the stacks of mangled metal look even more strange and ghostly. And it was freezing.

The bleating noise got even louder, closer, and underneath it, we heard the rumbling of thundering hooves that couldn't possibly belong to any animal that bleated. Cows? Horses? *Bulls?*

'Come on!' Sam yelled, and we turned back through everything we'd almost tripped over before, but this time covering the ground with desperate, panicked speed. I stumbled and crashed into Sam, blinded by the mist. He skidded on a fallen branch, and now a new noise blasted the air—

'*Naaaarr!*'

—and before I could even blink, they were on us, and they were goats. Only goats. But they were humongous, with long corkscrew horns that stuck up in the air, and they weren't stopping.

It was ear-shattering.

We sprinted back the way we'd come, but got lost and hit hedge. If there was anywhere to go, we couldn't see it. The goats closed in. All my breath seemed to stick in my throat.

'*Naaaarr!*'

I screamed at Sam, 'WHAT DO WE DO?' And he yelled back, 'SOMETHING MUST BE STALKING THEM!'

How did he know? But a second later, I thought I saw a flash of something extremely fast, whizzing through their feet. There was definitely a whiff of warm rubber in the air.

'Sam!' I yelled. 'I think I saw ...' But it ended in a cough as I got a goat shoulder to the chest.

The goats pushed and pushed till we were rammed against the hedge.

'Naaaarr!'

'Stay there!' Sam bawled.

'Won't we get squashed?'

He didn't answer. It was hard to think about anything but breathing. The goats' bawling filled our ears. Their footsteps were heavy and panicked. Yellow teeth bared with each vibrating 'Naaaarr'. Horns thwacked horns, far too close to us and far too colossal – their backs came up to my shoulder – and the air stank of wet goat. I tried to turn, desperate to get my face away from them, and eventually managed to get one arm out to cover my eyes, but it was impossible to move from the neck down AT ALL. We were pinned. The goats pressed us further and further into the hedge, and the sharpest bits of it stuck into our backs and legs. They were crushing us. We were going to suffocate.

My whole face was clammy with sweat. Wet seeped through my jeans. Breath floated around us, mixing with the mist, and – worse – some of them had let loose, in every way.

Then Sam must have found a space because suddenly he could move, and he was shooing them off us – 'Shift! Go on! *Get!*' – and stamping his feet. I was still completely pasted, and when the whole mass shifted, it was worse for me – they pushed and pushed, squashing me further in than ever, and I had no breath left to even wail. Sam stamped again. He kicked and roared at the top of his lungs, but the goats got all confused and stormed off again in total stampede mode – and Sam vanished.

I didn't see how – it happened too fast. One of the biggest goats must have got between us, and the only way for Sam not to be trampled was to go along with it.

'*Sam!*'

Then I saw him, bobbing in the goat-crowd. He shouted something, but it was drowned out by the bleating. Hurling myself after them did no good – I couldn't reach him. The whole procession blundered blindly on through the mist with me scrabbling after them, wading through tall ferns, skidding over stones and ignoring gashes from bricks and junk.

Sam was going to get crushed. How would I explain it to his mum and dad? To the ambulance people? It was all my fault.

We came out of the other side of the mist on to flatter ground. Never knew mist could have edges, but the rest of the garden was clear right up to the sky. The goats stopped and looked around in a daze, breathing hard and fast, stumpy tails twitching.

'Sam?'

I couldn't see him. He was nowhere. Dread leaked upwards from my knees, making my breathing shudder. Then something different moved in the middle of the herd and I saw his T-shirt. He stood up, brushed himself off and shook his drenched head. He looked normal but messed up, as if he'd been fighting, and the goats moved calmly out of his way. Everyone in the scene was dripping wet.

My heart thudded so hard. 'You OK?'

Sam nodded, and squeezed his ankle with both hands.

'Did they get you there?'

'It just got a bit twisted,' he snapped. 'It's nothing.'

It didn't sound like nothing. He brought his binoculars out and turned them over. They didn't look broken, but they didn't exactly look wonderful any more either. There were scuff marks on one side, and the strap looked a bit frayed.

'Sorry, Sam – unlucky. Phew …'

He glared at me and limped over to the goats.

'Let's get them penned up in here,' he barked farmer-ishly, and he pointed to a fenced-off corner of the field garden. 'Probably where they're meant to be.'

I looked around. We were behind the house, at the

opposite side to the trees. The goats scattered faster than Sam could round them up. I dived in front and headed them off, throwing my arms forward to make them go. It worked. Now they'd stopped panicking, they were actually quite good at doing what we wanted.

Sam took over for the last part. He fed them through the gateway of the little field, doing farmer movements and farmer whistles, then tied the broken gate fastening at the top and kicked it into place at the bottom. I tried to pull my wet and sticky jeans away from my legs, but they kept pinging back.

'Where'd you get the string?'

He tapped his pocket, saying nothing, and in a few minutes it was done: the goats were in, their gate was fastened, and we leaned against it, recovering.

'*You done herded those goats*,' I said, in my best American accent, 'but that was off-the-scale scary.' Mud and grass-juice were splotched down the front of his T-shirt. He didn't look at me at all. I tried again. 'You really OK? Cos you went down and everything. Thought you were toast.'

He stayed silent for a moment, and my whole chest felt like it was sinking into my stomach. How long was he going to stay mad with me?

But then he nodded and said, 'Yup – they just stepped over me,' on a big, amazed breath.

'Wow, properly majestic,' I said, and let out a big relieved sigh of my own. 'Did you see anything while you were down? Did you see what spooked them?' The creature didn't *seem* to be there now, but I was still suspicious.

He shook his head. 'Perhaps goats spook easy. I don't know goats.'

I looked at them. 'They're back to normal. Instantly!'

He nodded. Some headbutted each other gently, as if they didn't really mean it. Most ate grass. Only one of the adults still grumbled under her breath. Her kid answered in smaller, sadder, gurgling bleats, nostrils quivering like it had secret batteries up its nose. The rest acted like nothing had happened.

The mist started rolling away, a grey-white mass floating like a Zeppelin. Now the giant trees were visible again. We frowned at each other.

'The mist? And the goats? I think it was the thing from the box,' I said. 'I think I saw it.'

Sam was silent for a long time, like he didn't want to agree but couldn't find a reason not to. 'Put it in your records,' he said.

The sun came out and our shadows loomed up gigantic, but still the air was full of what had nearly happened.

As we walked away from the goats, things felt better. We'd been helpful. Back around the front, bright sunlight turned the empty windows of Ash House into silver plates. It was only old raindrops clinging on, but it looked magical. The creepy empty loneliness had faded off. The rushing, butting emergency was over. We even got a laugh when a tame moth landed on my hand.

'Hey, look at its face,' I said. 'Looks like it's got a handlebar moustache. The moths round here are *extreme*. He's got to be doing something to change them – you never normally see moths in the daytime.' The words jumbled together. Giggles nearly spilt out of me from total, brutal relief.

'Yeah, you do,' Sam said. 'They're not all nocturnal.'

Then there was a noise. Sam held up a warning hand, but I'd heard it. We stopped dead at the side of the house. The sound was feet. Shuffly, unsteady ones, but definitely footsteps on the jaggedy front path. Dislodging stones. Someone slow, but unstoppable, old-man-shaped, and very, very bossy. It was the boiled-egg-headed old man from the village hall.

His voice hit me like a slap. 'Well now. It's my duty, as head of the parish council, to check on problem areas in this village periodically – but what excuse do *you two* have to be here, eh? You're on private property, and the owner is quite clearly absent …'

'We were passing.' Breath seemed to catch in my throat. 'We heard some goats in trouble. We went to help, stopped them getting out on the road.'

He looked straight at me. His eyes were full of fake amazement that I really thought he'd believe anything that came out of my mouth. Cold eyes. Lizard eyes. He looked like he had a cold: bulgy, watery eyes and pinkish, sore-looking nostrils. The nostrils flared. 'Hey! You were at the jumble sale. Bit of a snooper all round, aren't you.'

Sam shrank towards the wall of the house 'You didn't tell me the old man was Mr Lombard,' he muttered.

I looked at my shoes and shrugged. How could I have known?

Lombard snorted in disgust and turned his back on me. He looked at Sam and folded his arms.

'Goats in trouble?' he said. 'Did their trouble come before or after you'd chased them round their pen, Sam Irwin?' His thin lips pressed together in a straight, mean line. He smelt of wet paint.

'No, we sorted them, Mr Lombard,' Sam said. His voice was high and squeaky and horrified. 'They were stampeding.'

'This is no place for youngsters like you. Knowing Clemm, he'll have parts of it electrified.' Mr Lombard spread the word 'electrified' on to the air, making it last far too long. The sun went in and it started raining again, in tiny, hurting needles. He glanced at me again, then said to Sam, 'You ought to be a bit choosier about the company you keep, Sam Irwin.'

I heated up all over, starting in my outraged cheeks. Sam looked like he might never move from that spot on the path again. I opened my mouth to protest at the injustice, but then something stopped me from thinking straight – a car was slowing down outside the drive, and I had a horrible feeling about it.

'Well, here's the man himself,' Mr Lombard said, and he scratched his raspy cheek. 'Let's see what he makes of your tale.'

It *was* him. The Bentley's tyres crunched over gravel. Windscreen wipers revealed the huge shape of Mr Clemm, whose furious eyes zipped between Mr Lombard, Sam and me, as if he couldn't decide which of us was worst.

Without really thinking about it, I started walking. There was no way out of the garden except past that horrific car, but also no way I was staying to have a nice little chat with Lombard AND the Cloaked Strider. I grabbed Sam by the arm and pulled him after me as I went for the Bentley head on.

I'd forgotten how gigantic Mr Clemm really is. I could hear my own heart beating. He filled the car, right to the roof. We speeded up, but we couldn't run – that would have looked like guilt on four legs. The rain fell in straight rods now.

'Oy!' Mr Lombard shouted. 'You two goons! Stay and face the music!'

My eyes met Mr Clemm's as we passed. That hawk face. So much nose. So much eagle-owl-eyebrow, puzzled, meeting in the middle, and his eyes, dark as night. I forgot to take a breath. This felt like falling in a nightmare. It felt like walking into a thick black spider's web, all in slow motion. Inside I cringed, expecting him to spring out of the car and yank hold of us both, one in each hand.

We dived out of the front gate and grabbed our bikes from the hedge. Impossible not to look back. Had to see if he'd follow.

Mr Clemm got out of the car like a bat unfolding itself.

We didn't stop pedalling till we reached the shop, and I've never been so soaked in my life. I did say sorry to Sam, for the way everything turned out. I did it just as we split to go our separate ways – Sam went up the hill to Lilac Farm and I went home to Usher's Place – but he didn't even look at me.

As we passed, the neon light over the shop flashed on for a second, then fizzed halfway between off and on before sputtering out again.

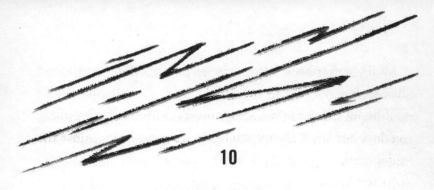

10

Malfunction

<u>6.15 p.m.</u>

It's the evening and I'm still shivering, even though I've changed and I'm sitting at the kitchen table and the cooker's going.

Lily went for me as soon as I got back here, while I was still sopping wet.

She grabbed me by the scruff of my soaking T-shirt and tried to drag me in to face Mum. I held on to the door frame with everything I had. Nothing would budge me, but Lily didn't stop trying.

'How can I be expected to look after things when Mum's at work if you keep doing exactly the opposite of what you're told?' she said, yanking hard on every third word. 'You've got *zero* respect for me.'

'Lily, you're in a total stress-out! You never used to get like this—'

She let go of me suddenly, and because I'd been pulling against her with all my strength, I went flying against the sideboard.

'Ow! You—'

'Hey, you two,' Mum called from the kitchen. 'What's going on in there?'

'It's Alfie!' Lily yelled.

'It's not, Mum!' I shouted. 'It's Lily! She's being tragic!'

Lily glared down at me. I couldn't see even a shadow of the old Lily. She used to be fun. If anyone in the house was reading a newspaper, she'd put her head down and charge at it like a bull. How long has it been since I saw her do that?

'You can't have your own way the whole time just because you've been bullied,' I said to her, getting up slowly and rubbing my bashed elbow. 'Anyway, you owe me.'

'Pretty sure I do *not*.'

'We all had to move here for *your* benefit. I wasn't even asked. And now you're not one bit grateful.'

She gave me another killer death glare and said, 'Don't be so ignorant! How would you like it if you could hardly swallow anything? You just gobble up everything in sight without even thinking about it.'

'Why should I think? It's only eating.'

'Oh you utter, utter piece of wastage,' she said, and lunged for me again.

Before Lily had her trouble, rowing meant secretly throwing each other's things out of the bedroom windows, or pouring each other's drinks away, or just a quick shouting match. But since, our rows have been more spectacular. She pulls and tugs and slaps. Dad says it's like someone's turned her into a human firework.

I twisted away from her and snapped her bracelet (by accident – it was her fault for grabbing me so viciously, and anyway, I've got fresh goat injuries) and started yelling at her to keep her nails out of my flesh and she was screaming back that she deserves respect and then Mum came in and started shouting at both of us and then I realised that the lights were getting brighter and brighter and brighter. I thought they'd pop for sure. We all looked up and went silent. And then they went back to normal.

Mum got over it quickest. 'Get to the table and not another word from the pair of you. We're eating *now*.'

Then Lily went back to her normal self too. 'I don't *want* your sweaty stew!'

'Lily, it's exactly the same one I made last week. You liked it then.'

'It's made with pure sweat!'

'Mum,' I said, 'can Lily stop being in charge while you're out? I was only with Sam, and she's acting like she owns me.'

That caused another volcanic eruption, and Lily stormed upstairs. As she went, the light above the stairs flickered, and I swear it went a pinky colour.

Mum sighed. 'She just wants to feel like she's got a bit of control *somewhere*. Bullying is complicated, Alfie. It does things to you that can't easily be undone.'

'Well maybe I'd understand better if you actually told me what happened to her,' I snapped. 'Why's it such a big secret?' Mum pursed her lips together but didn't say anything because right then the kettle randomly switched itself on.

I think the thing from the box has followed me home.

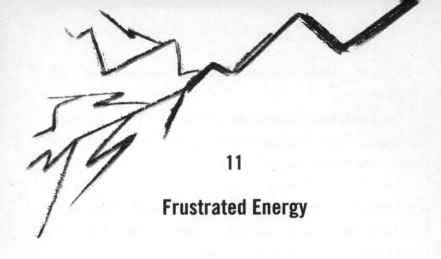

11

Frustrated Energy

The last day of term. Sam and I have just walked from the school bus full of supercharged zip. The whole summer holidays are here: aeons of time for what's shaping up into a mega investigation.

'Hey, the giant guinea pigs are real animals,' Sam told me, rubbing his hands together with immense satisfaction. 'They're called capybara. They're the size of a small pig.'

'Waaay! Imagine that stampede! Spitting frogs are real too, I'm sure of it. But listen,' I said, making fast mini-skids in some gravel with my shoes. 'This morning, when I was getting milk out of the fridge, the whole thing convulsed.'

'Fridges are always juddering. It's just the compressor—'

'No – this was really radical rattling. It was practically rocking.'

Sam screwed up his eyes doubtfully. 'What did your mum say when it did that?'

'She didn't see it.'

He snorted. 'It's pointless repeating what we did yesterday.'

'I'm telling you, it's definitely in the house with me. We just need to get stealthier. We'll sit still in my room till the creature gets bored and comes out.'

Yesterday after school, Sam and I had spent hours looking for it. We tried everything. We turned on every single appliance in the house till Mum went mad and sent us to the shop to get eggs she didn't even need, but all we found was two hot plug sockets and a digital clock that thought the time was 99:99. You'd think the creature was hiding itself away from Sam. So annoying. I need him to believe me.

'You don't even know for sure if that box had anything alive in it. What if you just saw a spark, some static, a surge of electricity shooting out? There'll be a simple scientific explanation for everything that looks weird up there.'

My heart started racing. 'I've *told* you – it was definitely some kind of creature. *No way* was it just a spark!' I said. 'And that box is a massively important part of this whole mystery. The moths on it – trillions of them, there were – they're something to do with it. Maybe electricity attracts them too, like light.'

'But moths can be quite weird anyway,' Sam said. 'Nature is amazing all by itself – you don't need to imagine any magical weirdness on top.'

He sounded a bit pompous now. Everything has to have a tedious scientific explanation. I was about to tell him to stop droning on – because he can – but a second later, he blew my mind.

'Some types of moth don't even have a mouth.'

I stopped walking. 'What? How do they *eat*?'

'They don't. They ate everything they were ever going to eat while they were caterpillars. That type aren't adults for long. No time to eat.'

'That's insane! Astonishingly, pulsatingly insane!' I said, as we walked up the path to my house. 'You're wasting your brain, Sam. You could sell that info.'

In the hallway Sam stopped dead, frowning.

'I mean it,' I blathered on. 'I'm sure you could get a few quid from teachers – think how much more interesting they could make their lessons. And online magazines would definitely buy your know-how—'

Sam silenced me with a pointing finger. 'Your rotten coat!'

Slung over the banister, like an awful premonition of doom, was my terrible puffer coat. My whole head went obscenely hot.

Lily came out of the kitchen. She folded her arms and had a good nosy as I inspected the ugly thing and hung it on its peg.

'Mr Fuming brought that back, Mum says. You know, the old shouty-crackers man from the village hall? Mum's gone to help set up tonight's concert,' she said, keeping her face completely blank. 'Where d'you leave it? How does he know where you live?'

I didn't look at Sam, but felt waves of horror coming off him. This was the worst-case scenario. Now Mr Lombard, of all people, would know I had been to Ash House before the goats.

'Were you here?' I asked her. 'What did he say?'

She shrugged. 'Saw him with my eyes. Didn't speak to him with my mouth.'

_5.30 p.m._

We've both calmed down, but Sam's gone into quiet mode. He's jumpy. I've tried to tell him he'll be fine – Mr Lombard is bound to notice me because I'm the only brown person round here besides Lily and Dad and that old lady at the village hall. Sam doesn't stand out at all.

But now we have to go to this lame end-of-term concert at the village hall, and he's spooked about it because with my coat turning up on top of the goat incident, evidence is mounting up. Apparently *everyone* goes to this concert when the schools break up – it's one of those things that happens in the village, and you can't get out of it. Our mums are doing the refreshments for the interval, so me and Sam are doubly doomed. We have to help.

8.30 p.m.

I'm back. What a night! Still can't believe it.

At first, it was dire. Little kids sang and played instruments and parents wore numbskullingly sickening smiles. So boring. Until the music stopped. That's when everything started happening, out of absolutely *nowhere*. The first thing was that Mr Lombard climbed on to the stage and cleared his throat like a very important walrus.

'The parish council has received reports of children trespassing in village gardens. Newcomers to our village need to listen very carefully: this is not the way we do things in Folding Ford. We *do not* trespass on private property. The police have already been informed, so those problem elements amongst you need to take note.'

A few faces turned to stare at me. How did they know? Sam poked me in a *told-you-so* way.

Mum turned to me too, with this horrified look, and mouthed, '*Problem elements?*' I felt sweat breaking out on my forehead and at the roots of my hair, and everyone started whispering, and the heat in my brain felt like it might blow the top of my head straight off.

And that's exactly when rain started pelting against the windows, as if someone was hurling buckets of water at the glass, sideways. Wind howled somewhere near the roof, circled lower and louder, then whined through every crack in the room. It almost felt like *I* was doing it – it completely matched how I was feeling.

Every single staring person forgot about me and gawped at the storm instead. There were *Oohs* and *Wows* as everyone stood up and went to the window for a closer look.

I took deeper breaths and calmed down and – so spine-tinglingly strange – so did the storm outside. No rain, no wind. The sun came out. It was the weirdest thing in this whole sea of weird. Sam was staring at me. But now the air felt very warm and close to my skin. Heavy air. Tricky air. People sighed and complained about how stuffy it was.

'Did you see what happened?' I said to Sam. 'Tell me that wasn't weird. It *had* to be the creature. Did you see the whole storm thing reacting to me?'

'I saw … I'm not sure. It was peculiar. What did you do?'

'I just relaxed and the storm stopped.'

'But how …?'

I shrugged. 'It was masterful. Insane! Nearly wet myself!'

But then Mum rounded us up to help with the refreshments. 'Collect all the used beakers you can see, please, Alfie,' she said. 'Use a tray. Then go into the kitchen and start washing them up.' She still looked at me slightly suspiciously, as if she was trying to work out exactly who Mr Lombard's *problem elements* might be.

'Wash up?' I said. 'Don't they get chucked?'

'They're recyclable beakers,' said Mum, menacingly. 'They're indestructible.'

Sam helped.

'Quick as we can,' I said. 'We've got a mystery to solve.'

We ditched the boring trays so the beakers could be stacked more ingeniously. Sam worked fast, but I was a tornado. Soon, both of us had a tower of beakers in each hand and could only get them back to the kitchen at top speed by balancing perfectly.

Which was when I almost ran into Mr Lombard.

'*Alfie!*' Mum snapped. 'Sorry, Mr Lombard.'

He raised his eyebrows and switched his stare between Mum's white face and my brown one, as if he thought she might have found me on the street.

Lily was in the kitchen leaning against a radiator. I pointed my finger at her. 'Hey – why aren't you doing jobs?'

She glared at me, opened her hand and put a biscuit in her mouth.

I whispered to Sam, 'Look at that! Lily! With a biscuit! My sister never eats biscuits.'

He looked at me sideways, and tipped the beakers into the sink. I suppose you don't get it unless you've had a sister who's nearly starved to death. He hasn't even got a sister.

'Why does a biscuit matter?' he whispered.

I sighed. 'It's not just the biscuit – it's the whole thing. She got bullied – nearly to death. She was too upset to eat. And now ...' I pointed at Lily with my head.

He was trying to analyse it, I could see. Heaps of people have tried to do that and got nowhere. 'She's getting better? And you think it's because you moved here?'

'Maybe,' I said. 'But it's been months and she hasn't eaten a biscuit before. Hey! Brains run on electricity, right? Maybe the creature's changing all our brains!'

'Pah!' He smirked and shook his head and put the plug in the sink.

I studied Lily again, then left Sam with the beakers. 'Lily … do you feel different since we moved here?'

'*What?*'

'Lily, you're eating a *biscuit*.'

'*Such* detective skills,' she snapped, and left the room.

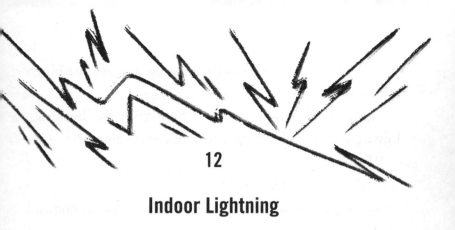

12

Indoor Lightning

We *started* washing up. Mum probably wouldn't believe it, but we did turn the tap on and would have squirted in washing-up liquid if this monster fizzing noise hadn't ripped across the ceiling at that exact second. The strip-light above our heads suddenly brightened and a dazzling ball of brilliant white light – like a mini sun – hurtled from one end of the tube to the other.

We ducked and darted to the other side of the room just as a sizzling zigzag of lightning shot from the tube to the ground, leaving a silver trail in my eyes.

I turned to Sam. '*What?* How …?'

'Got a retinal after-image!' he said.

'Yeah, that. Me too. Lightning *inside*!'

The tube exploded. Powdered glass drifted to the floor.

'Whoa, Sam! It's raining glass.'

A sour battery-acidy smell curled up my nose, and then Mum was beside us.

'*Look!*' I said, pointing to the glass with one hand and the ceiling with the other. My heart was hammering in my ears.

'The tube has blown,' Mum said. 'Come away. I'll get Mr Lombard – come right out of here.'

'Mum, this lightning bolt rippled across the ceiling and zoomed into the light tube and bounced around like a comet and then – *boom!* The tube exploded! And now the air's gone all heavy – can't you feel it?'

Mum frowned. 'Is there some exaggeration to subtract from that, Alfie, or are you saying it straight?'

'It's straight up, Mrs Bradley,' Sam said. 'Like when hot air ripples off the pavement when it's uber-hot –' he stared at the space with wide eyes – 'except this went sideways.'

'Dina, Sam,' Mum said. 'You can call me Dina. Lightning inside the tube?' She opened and closed her mouth a few times to show how hard she was trying to believe us. (She always thinks fish-faces help with this.) 'There's certainly thunder on the way – the air's very oppressive. After that rainstorm earlier, I'm surprised it hasn't cleared. My head feels terrible, but the weather just needs to break. That's all that's going on, boys.'

I looked at Sam. He spiked his hair with his hand and blinked.

'Actually, you two go and tell Mr Lombard,' Mum said, 'and I'll deal with this glass.'

The next big thing happened in the main hall, which was now in meltdown. As soon as Sam and I opened the door, we felt a wave of hot outrage escaping, and the noise was unbelievable. Almost every single person in that room seemed to be arguing.

My sister was standing with her back against the wall, pretending to be cool, while parents tried to sort kids out, standing between fighting ones, holding back shoving ones, and it was impossible to work out what had started it. Sam and Roan's mum is called Cindy. She stood red-faced in the middle with my mum, and warring kids swirled around them. Mum looks so funny when she's helpless; it was murder trying to keep my face straight.

'Sick!' Sam said. 'That thing you let loose must be strapping!'

The air was getting even heavier.

'Feels exactly like a thunderstorm,' Sam said, wiping the sweat off his face.

I nodded. 'The weather weirdness has definitely got more intense since I let that thing out of its box. We need to think happy thoughts to calm it down.'

'What? Why?'

'When Mr Lombard said all that stuff, the weather got worse, just like it was matching my feelings. So if both of us concentrate on generating good feelings ...?'

He shrugged. 'OK then.'

'Happy thoughts,' I said, humming. 'I'm thinking of going trampolining with Lily. We used to do that loads. What are you thinking about?'

He shook his head at me. 'You're making too much noise for anyone else to think at all!'

I pulled my best monster face and dug my elbows in his ribs till he laughed. I think it started working, because Sam's little brother Roan had been in the middle of the row, but now he left the person he'd been arguing with and weaved between the bodies instead, moving his neck like a chicken and laughing his head off. The heat in the room lifted slightly. Someone opened a window. Sam laughed in amazement and gave me a thumbs-up.

In less than a minute a youth club leader came in and started sending everyone home. We went to get our coats while our mums collected their baskets of supplies – but then something rumbled behind the cloakroom wall. There was a tearing sound. The floor vibrated, and so did my legs.

We spoke together. 'It's in the walls!'

13

Cosmic Background Radiators

Sam and I stepped backwards, feeling our way to the cloakroom entrance without taking our eyes off the wall. We hardly breathed. Out in the main corridor, kids still clattered around.

Something scraped along inside the wall. My hair roots tingled, and Sam's hair lifted by itself – way up in the air.

'It's following you, Alfie!' Sam said.

I pulled a puzzled face.

'It's going wherever you are!'

The noise stopped, as if it was listening to us.

'Alfie, let's go.'

'Wait!'

The bottom of the wall bubbled like the topping on a pizza in the oven. Was it coming out?

Sam pulled my arm. 'You maniac! It's dangerous!'

I shook him off. 'Won't hurt us – could have done that by now. It knows I let it out. It's listening to us.' To me.

'I'm getting your mum.'

He legged it, and for the next few silent seconds, me and the creature were alone again.

The coats in front of me rippled, and one slipped off its peg. That sour smell came back. Where the wall met the floor, a swirl of dusty smoke drifted from a tiny gap, like a shadow—

Lily was suddenly beside me. Before I could stop her, she'd thrown something at the smoke.

'*No!*' I snatched at her hand too late.

Red liquid ran down the wall. A massive arc of blue light shot from the gap to where Lily's hand had been a second before.

CRACK! The sound came a moment later, like the air was breaking apart.

Then nothing.

Lily stepped back and wiped her trembling hands on her trousers, breath quivery, face pale.

I gripped both her arms. 'You could have been killed!'

'It was only blackcurrant juice. I smelt burning.'

I glared at her, squeezing her arms hard. I couldn't

stop, even when the others came back. Mum pulled us apart.

Then, instead of yelling at me – which I expected – Lily hugged me.

I could feel her heart beating like crazy, and a warm feeling started in the roots of my hair. We pulled away and looked at each other, both of us doing that smiley-frown thing. I was *so* glad she hadn't been hurt. The relief felt like a weight coming off my chest – the everyday Lily-ness of her suddenly mattered more than my creature.

We left just as Mr Lombard arrived, frowning between me and the burn marks.

9.30 p.m.

Now I've got over the shock of Lily nearly being zapped, I want to go back to the village hall. Mum bundled us off home before I could check that wall again – there was no time to even listen for any movement. Has Lily killed it? Would water kill an electric creature? *Water and electricity don't mix* – that's so obvious and vital, and I can't get it out of my head. The wall was hot and steaming.

And Lily actually hugged me! That's so random. Maybe the old Lily is still in there somewhere.

Sam just texted me:

Sam: _You awake? Seen anything else?_
Me: _All quiet here. Maybe my sister's killed it. Water +_
electricity = pain
Sam: _Maybe. Or could be injured …_
Me: _Oh no!_
Sam: _And it travels through wires. So must be able_
to compress like a digital signal, then unzip at the
other end

(See, that's clever. Keeping Sam in full science mode brings
excellent results. That first biology lesson when we became
mates, he told me there's a certain spider that drinks with
its bum. It sucks rocks to get liquid out. With its bum. See?
How could you know stuff like that and not make money?
How could you keep it all in? Sometimes I think Sam's
like a sponge. You squeeze him, and little facts dribble out.
Time to get squeezing.)

Me: _Weird how it was still changing the weather from_
inside that box
Sam: _Maybe it was uncomfortable. Thrashing about._

	Spewing out some kind of interference. Electrical things do that
Me:	*We need a name for it. How about Electro-Dude?*
Sam:	*Terrible*
Me:	*Current Kid*
Sam:	*Awful!*
Me:	*Wired-o*
Me:	*Flashy*
Me:	*Electron Ron*
Me:	*Lightning Rod … Sparky*
Sam:	*Whizzy*

I smiled. *Excellent!*

14

The Wasteland

Midnight

Mum went to bed ages ago. Can't settle.

I'm getting up.

12.45 a.m.

Unreal.

Got up, but instead of going downstairs I looked out of the window, otherwise none of it would have happened.

The glass was wet – it must have just finished raining. Everything was shiny. I leaned my forehead against the window to feel its coolness – and saw a movement.

In the wasteland opposite our house, a glowing glimmer of light pulsed. We call it the wasteland, but really, it's going to be another house. It's a building plot, and the owners dug out the foundations, then left it to grow weeds and brambles. You couldn't build anything on it now without starting again. Dad says they ran out of money. So what was that glimmer? It shouldn't be there, so – could it be Whizzy?

Silently, on a huge breath, I got dressed, crept downstairs and let myself out of the house. I went out the back way: the kitchen door unlocks smoothly and opens with a silent handle, but it was still risky. Until not very long ago, Mum used to check Lily's room at intervals all through the night, like she was a baby. She could wake at the slightest noise.

The air outside felt perfect: cool but not cold. Mum's window reflected a three-quarter moon, but there were no stars showing. Our garden was mostly black shapes. Couldn't see what lurked there and hadn't brought a torch. Everything was so still. Too still. My heart beat *so* fast. Did I really dare?

Across the road, I swear the wasteland had got thicker and blacker and more wasted. The colossal weed-mountain felt far too close. I climbed it months ago when it was just an abandoned soil heap. Now it's covered in tall, spiky weed-flowers, and they quivered like a wind I couldn't feel was tickling them all over.

Different shades of darkness mapped out the shape of each weed against the sky. I smelt weeds and soil and fizzing secrets, and looked back across the road at our house. How many steps would it take to reach my bed? Thirty? More? Then it happened.

The air was suddenly hot, as if someone had turned on a gas cooker. Something sizzled. Way above my head in the power lines, there was a humming, as if the electricity inside them wanted out.

A gust of wind rushed straight at me. At the top of the weed-mountain, a small, bright shape swirled in and out of sight. Seconds later, the shape came rippling down the mountain towards me, getting bigger and trailing threads of light. Whizzy!

My hands grabbed for something to hold on to and found a rickety fencepost. My legs were jelly, but I couldn't run away. Couldn't miss this.

Whizzy shimmered and twisted silently. Whizzy was ripples and curves of light, in no definite shape at first. My hair lifted. My scalp tingled. A scorched smell rose from the ground. Whizzy pushed through the air, as if the air was as thick as water, and in just another second, Whizzy was closer and much bigger. My heart beat hard.

It was rubbish at staying balanced. Every time the top moved, the rest made a little ripple to get steady again, but when it did, when I finally got a clear look at it, my heart stopped racing quite so fast. My lips curled into a smile and my mouth opened wide in a silent gasp at the total, magnificent, extreme brilliance of it: my wonderful, impossible electrical creature.

Looks like it's mostly made of white light. Its head curves over in an S-shape like a horse's, but kind of not. And it has eyes! Shiny discs of the darkest silver anywhere, ever.

A row of quivery semicircular things down its sides ripple like gills the whole time, and there are no arms or legs, just like a seahorse. It's a bendy, wavy stalk of light with glowing, golden insides that look like they're silently crackling with electricity—

And it looked at me like I was just as full-on amazing.

Silence. The wires above were quiet now. Every sizzle and buzz had stopped.

That smell again: sour old batteries, burned rubber – the exact smell from the cloakroom walls at the concert. My teeth fizzed and itched like mad. I had to rub my gums. This close, I could see why the eyes shone: they're like mirrors. You can see things reflected in them. I saw the moon. Clever. Unbelievable.

No mouth under those eyes, though. No mouth at all.

Slowly, I let go of the post and lifted both hands in front

of my chest, palms out. In my mind, Sam's voice said, *Electricity can jump!* But I had to make some kind of greeting. My breathing slowed to normal and the last scraps of fear melted. Even so, my hands and the tip of my nose felt like they were close to a candle, and a shuddery feeling went down both arms to my elbows, as if I'd banged my funny bones. A nicer, fireworky smell came off Whizzy now.

Can't believe I wasn't scared, but when something's scary, the fear travels down your back in ripples. This was the opposite. My skin felt safe all over. Didn't feel like Whizzy wanted to hurt me – at least, not on purpose. It was jumpy, like a nervous puppy. Ready to disappear in a second if it needed to. Scared of me, but curious. Totally *curious*.

The weirdest part was trying to work out how long it was, because the tail kept changing from short to long, like a flickering flame. Did that mean my eyes weren't even seeing it properly?

Then Whizzy dropped to the ground and spread horizontally for almost a minute, which was doubly cool. After that, before I could work out what was happening, Whizzy shot upwards in a perfect vertical streak that ended in a blur, as if the actual air had folded up. Whizzy was gone.

A patch of pale grey ash lay on the ground where Whizzy had been. I brushed one finger into the soft, warm, almost-wet powder. It smelt like singed hair. Then I stood there for ages. My eyes wouldn't go back to normal: a dark after-image made curvy lines behind my eyelids. *Wow*. I kept whispering it. *Wow*. I shook my head, couldn't believe it.

The house felt warm after the night air. Quiet, too, until I got halfway up the stairs just now. Lily was standing there looking down at me.

'I'm telling.' Her voice was a thin whisper.

My head still buzzed. I shook it at her. 'Couldn't sleep,' I whispered back. 'Just went outside to get cool.'

'No you didn't.' She smirked. 'It isn't even hot. You've been further than that.'

How much had she seen?

'Wandering about in the middle of the night,' she said. 'Wonder what Dad would say?'

'You bin your breakfast sometimes. I'll tell Mum that.' It came out fast, before I'd had the chance to think about it.

She stared down at me with cold eyes.

'I'll show her where you bury it in the compost,' I said.

She didn't move a muscle.

'The exact spot. I'll text Dad too.'

'That was once, and it was months ago,' she said.

'There'll be rats in the garden soon, and it'll be your fault. You're not supposed to dump cooked food in the compost.'

'Die in a hole,' she said, and spun into the bathroom, faster than I've ever seen her move.

Her words seemed to fly around the room for a second before stinging me in the face. Should have kept my mouth shut. When she'd hugged me after the concert, it felt like the real Lily was back. Now I'd ruined it.

I stood there for a minute listening to the leaves rustling against the landing window and trying to find that magical bubble-feeling I'd floated on out there with Whizzy, but it was gone.

Back in my room, I took one last look at the wasteland from my window in case Whizzy had returned. And that's when I saw it. A figure stood in the shadow of our beech tree. A figure so tall and elongated, it felt like he could easily reach up and prod a finger against my window. It had to be him. *The Cloaked Strider!*

And what was *that*? A black shadow hopped from his shoulder to the branches above him. Flappy. Fast. Some kind of bird? A bat?

He stared up at our house with eyes that glinted like glass.

He must have been watching the whole time.

He's found us.

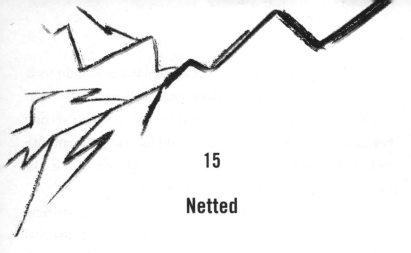

15

Netted

I'm back in bed, but feel all shaky. Not going to be able to sleep. Can't get Lily's face out of my head – why did I say those things? And the Cloaked Strider. He makes me shiver. What's he going to do? But everything else is zipping around my brain too. Wait till Sam hears about tonight! We're a team now that he believes me. We'll be unbeatable.

_1.30 a.m._

Sleep's not happening. Started copying this journal ready to send Dad these new creature sightings, and that's when it hit me: DELETE. It felt so wrong. DELETE, DELETE. I've been blabbing my mouth off when what I really needed to do was shut up. Sending these journal highlights to Dad was a rubbish idea – this journal is like dynamite. If Dad starts focusing and believes me, he might put a stop to the whole thing. He might even tell somebody, and then everyone in the world will come to Folding Ford, and my amazing creature could get captured again. Going to stop sending. Going to start being really careful about what I say to *absolutely everyone*. Except Sam.

26th July, 5.00 p.m.

This morning I started wolfing breakfast, but phoned Sam with my gigantic news before I'd even finished my toast – just had to. I sneaked the whole plate back up to my room – with an extra handful of chocolate rice.

I was telling him how Whizzy had stretched out huge, then compressed. 'I reached out and it seemed kind, it—'

'What?' he said. 'You buffoon! You can't touch it. You could've been electrocuted!'

'It doesn't mean any harm,' I said. 'I can tell.'

'You clot! It might not mean to, but you'd be just as dead. Electricity will try to find earth – through *you*, if you're the quickest way.'

And then something happened. It started in my half-empty water glass. A miniature whirlwind tumbled inside it, whipping the water into little peaks.

'Alfie?'

'Yeah, just a—'

Something bright shot past my bedroom window and I looked outside. Lily had gone out there in a mood earlier because it was her turn to take the washing off the line. But when I saw her my breath caught in my throat. She was dancing. She'd dumped the washing in the basket and turned her face up to the sky. Her arms were outstretched, her eyes closed, and she was turning slowly, swaying one way, then another. It took a moment for me to work out why the edges of her hair were glistening, and then I looked up at the sky. A stack of those freakish pancake clouds floated high above her, all by themselves. Lily stuck out her tongue and then I got it: she always sticks her tongue out in the rain. Those clouds were raining on her – fine, misty, almost-not-there rain. My heart started a panicky beat: if those clouds were made by Whizzy, then what would their rain do to Lily?

'Hello?' Sam said. 'You still there?'

'Yeah, wait. Something's happening.'

A soft swirl of pale pink light now whirled in circles around Lily's ankles. Hard to see unless you happened to be especially looking, and even then, it disappeared totally for ages at a time. I concentrated on it. Dad calls this 'getting your eye in'. The light was *so* weak and as thin as a piece of sewing thread. No wonder Lily couldn't feel it. But then she opened her eyes, stopped dancing and looked around. Quicker than a flash, Whizzy dived to the top of the tree and whizzed to a blur before cleverly vanishing. Lily didn't see a thing. The tree had moths, though – flurries of them flew around the top of it in excited little balls, and Lily did see those and began jumping up and down and calling for Mum.

Why was Whizzy so interested in Lily? Was it something to do with her throwing that juice? I went cold at the thought ... but Whizzy had looked more curious than angry just now—

'Alfie?'

At *exactly* the same time as Sam spoke my name, Whizzy shot in through my open window, zoomed downstairs in a split second and was outside again before I could take a single breath.

'Whizzy's back,' I told him. 'Whizzy is happening.'

'What, now?' Sam said, almost squeaking. 'Wait, I'll bike down! Keep it there, can you? Till I get there?'

'I'll try.'

I went outside to get a better look, and now it was much easier. Whizzy was using the chimney too. In, out, round and round, shimmering coils of light pink. Was Whizzy pink forever now? It was a stunning colour.

Was Whizzy playing? Wild laughter bubbled up in my chest – but my next step nearly ended in disaster: Mr Clemm's bald cat was suddenly under my feet at the garden gate. I'd almost stepped on her.

'How on earth have you got down here?' I whispered, crouching to stroke her. She stared up at me with her strange, bare eyes as if she was trying to understand something – and then I had a horrible thought: if Whizzy was here, and the cat was here …

And right at that moment, a big car rolled around the corner at the other end of Usher's Place and I knew. It had to be him. My tummy crunched in on itself.

I shot back inside the house and phoned Sam from my room, but before he picked up, I went to the window. Outside our house, right next to the front gate, stood Mr Nathaniel Clemm. And he was having a really good look. I shrank back into the curtain. My chest felt like a tight knot of squashed-down panic.

Mr Clemm looked frustrated. Whizzy was visible again, and running rings around him: hiding, then appearing, then hiding again, still playing the same game. Mr Clemm glared at thin air, because as soon as he found Whizzy, it vanished. There were even circular flashes behind me, like pieces of moonlight come to life, but it was hardly worth turning my head before they were gone.

Now I totally got it all. Whizzy is attracted to me because I set it free. Mr Clemm was here to marmalise me for tampering with his stuff.

'Yep?' said Sam. 'I'm nearly at the river bridge.'

'He's come back for me! Mr Clemm's *here again*!'

My mind scrambled over a hundred frantic thoughts. There would be accusations of trespassing, maybe even damage. Criminal damage? I felt sick.

'No way! Right. Think. You need to hide.'

'What? But everyone knows I'm home!'

'That won't matter if they can't find you.' Sam sounded out of breath. 'The Cloaked Strider will give up and go home. Think of a place.'

I dived into the big walk-in junk cupboard in the spare room and got behind a box of old Lego, but it was no good. I started to smell hot metal, but couldn't work out where it was coming from. The lightbulb in the ceiling flashed on, fizzed noisily, then went off. While I was around, so was Whizzy.

I texted Sam – *Can't last in this hiding place* – and dived back to my room.

Mr Clemm had something over his shoulder: a stiff, bulky bag, almost like a picnic cool box. He swayed it from side to side, and I realised what it was: a contraption in disguise. He was trying to attract Whizzy with it. Why else would anyone hold an empty picnic box open in that way? He was trying to recapture Whizzy!

For a few eye-popping seconds, I was gripped. But Whizzy wasn't going inside that box. Whizzy was whizzing. Whizzy was turning Mr Clemm's head into Saturn, with Whizzy as the rings.

I phoned Sam again.

'OK, you're going to have to escape,' he said, 'and hope Whizzy follows. Try to lead Whizzy to safety.'

'But Mr Clemm'll see me. We need to distract him.'

'We?'

'Yes! Can you do it?'

Sam went silent for ages.

'Sam? Please?'

'I'm not getting mixed up in this stuff again—'

'*Please* Sam! Yours is the only brain that can get me and Whizzy out of this.'

He said nothing.

'A distraction. An expert distraction – the cleverest,' I said. 'Sam?'

'Yisss,' he said, sounding breathy. 'Still thinking.'

And rushing. He was definitely rushing. That gave me hope.

'Electricity's weird again.' It was Lily, thundering up the stairs. 'Lights keep coming on when they're meant to be off. And there are moths everywhere.'

'Yep.' Whizzy was getting stronger. Definitely. Which was probably not good.

Lily barged in and looked out the window with me.

'You're hiding from him, aren't you?' she said, giggling softly. 'You're hiding from your giant.'

'Don't be stupid.'

'Why don't you go and meet him if you're so obsessed? Instead of just spying?' Waves of Mum's perfume wafted off her.

'I'm not and I wasn't,' I said. 'I'm on my way to Sam's.'

'From here? Great route. Leaving by window? Bored with doors?'

'Fun*n*y.'

Lily's hair rose at the edges with static electricity, but she hadn't noticed. 'What's he doing here?'

I swallowed. 'Who knows?

She gave me a long suspicious look. And then the doorbell rang.

I froze.

Lily practically threw herself down the stairs but Mum had already opened the door, and all I could do was listen on stair number eleven, out of sight, and wait for the Cloaked Strider to ask Mum if she could please get her son …

'So sorry to bother you –' Mr Clemm's voice was all gentlemanly – 'but I wondered, with all this electrical chaos going on, if you might be able to make use of a generator.'

I was trapped.

Sprinted back up the stairs to my room and called Sam again.

'At bottom of Beggar's Hill,' he panted.

So all I could do was wait. I spied while I waited, but it was like spying on a car crash.

Had to endure the sight of Mum, Lily and Mr Clemm back out in the garden looking at the house. Lily looking super interested while Mr Clemm and Mum talked. Neither Mum nor Lily noticed Whizzy looping around the treetops, but I could tell Mr Clemm did.

Mr Clemm's mouth talked, but his eyes still scanned our house, searching everywhere, which sent scary chills down my spine, because he'd know I was in here.

Call from Sam: 'OK, I'm nearly at Usher's Place. Get ready to move. Don't let anyone see you, but wait till I text.'

I leaped into action and crept down to the kitchen in excellent stealth mode. Opened the back door almost silently, ducked under the window and along the wall perfectly … then jumped out of my skin at a loud voice behind me.

'Oh, Alfie, you're just so innocent, aren't you?' It was Lily. 'I'm not sure how you even stand it. What exactly are you doing here?'

'Get lost,' I hissed.

'He won't bite, you know. He's only asking about our electrics. He's an expert.' She said this last part so smugly that I could have dropped a fat, wriggly spider down her back. (If I'd had one.) 'And that freak-show cat belongs to him! She's called Julia. She's meant to have hair, actually. It all fell out one day, or something. Doesn't bother her, though.'

So Sam was right: the cat – Julia – had been electrified. Lily looked absolutely crazy-happy at her discovery.

'Right then,' she said, 'I'm going to tell Mum that … let's see … you're inspecting the drains? Or you need emotional help?'

And then Sam did his supreme act of distraction.

At first, his voice came from far away. Then it grew closer and his words were clear enough for me to know this was my only chance to leg it – *There's a massive animal loose on Halfway Lane! Quick!'* – and things got frantic. Everyone ran up the road to see what was happening, and … I made a dash for it.

The bottom of our garden seemed the safest exit. (Awkward – bins, fences and gravel piles round the back of these houses.) Had to travel like a bullet in case anyone saw me leaving – especially Mr Clemm. Criss-crossed scrubland, fields, and ended up taking an extreme bendy sideways route round the utter outskirts of Folding Ford.

I stopped once to make sure Whizzy was following, but only dared risk a few seconds. My teeth had been fizzy even before I left our garden, so I'd hoped Whizzy had stayed close, but it wasn't until I reached the bottom of Beggar's Hill that all the tiny hairs on my arms started to prickle and stand up straight like they'd been electrified. There was a smell of scorched rubber. Whizzy was definitely here. But where? And how about Sam?

I phoned him, walking and looking over my shoulder the whole time, but there was no answer.

And then Whizzy appeared, properly and totally.

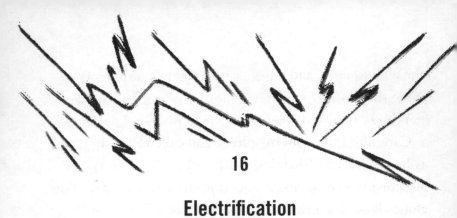

16

Electrification

This time, Whizzy was about my size and hovered centimetres from the ground. Behind it, tiny things fluttered. I couldn't make them out properly – Whizzy was too bright – but I guessed they were moths.

The folded layers of light. The graceful head with those seahorse curves that don't stay still long enough for you to really focus. Wow – Whizzy is the most beautiful thing I've ever seen. Is this why some people think there are angels?

'Whizzy,' I whispered. My breath was unbelievably trembly. 'Please hide. Neither of us are safe.'

But Whizzy didn't understand.

'This way, Whizzy,' I said. 'We need to get off the road and out of sight.'

I sprinted down a footpath that leads to the river. It's

one of our places, and there's a huge abandoned electricity pylon that doesn't work any more.

Whizzy followed.

Carefully, I took out my phone and called Sam, and just as he picked up, Whizzy skyrocketed up into the sky too fast for my eyes to follow. A little stack of pale pancake clouds floated almost exactly above my head.

'Sam, where are you? Get to the pylon now! Whizzy's here!'

'Coming! Just left Malusky's Corner. Please make it stay this time! What's it doing?'

'It's a scribble of pink in the sky! It's brilliant!'

A second later, Whizzy was down again. My phone was strangely warm, and it throbbed. The air smelt a bit burned, and a tiny rumble of baby thunder – the gentlest possible – sounded very close.

'What now?' Sam said, between fast, jerky breaths. 'Tell me!'

'The size keeps changing. It's gone really long – it stretches out metres and metres behind. Now it's small – only as long as my arm.'

Whizzy hung steadily in the air like a candle flame and seemed to throw curiosity at me like handfuls of sand. I stood still as we tried to work each other out.

'Its lower half looks different today – thick and

wavy, like melted glass. You can't see much of the fiery insides.'

'Yep, yep,' Sam said, panting.

Whizzy dived to the ground, making me jump, then spread out wide and long.

'It's wobbling like a washing machine doing a spin!'

Something sizzled. Was Whizzy getting energy from the ground?

A few raindrops fell and I took a step back. Water plus electricity equals nothing good. But what would happen when water hit Whizzy? I found out immediately: fizzing, mostly.

'Where are you?' I said to Sam. 'Get here! You have to see what it's doing to these raindrops!'

Each raindrop turned into a different fizzing colour. Soon there were loads of them, more colours than I even knew: a bluey green, a purplish red, an orangey yellow; all the colours were in between. Each drop of coloured rain then fell away separately, like a fountain made of tiny particles. This went on for about a minute before I realised Whizzy was doing it on purpose. For me? The noise was crazy.

'It's like Whizzy *loves* the rain!' I shouted down the phone line. 'Like rain is a new, cool thing! Sam? You there?'

The call was still active, but if he was answering, I couldn't hear him.

'You're like a piece of the sun,' I whispered to Whizzy. 'A true sunhorse.'

Whizzy stared, and I saw myself in those mirror eyes.

The air smelt hot and fireworky, even through the rain. Heat poured on to my face and my elbows tingled with that funny-bone feeling, and so did my teeth. I had to bite down hard to control it. We could never touch, me and Whizzy, but maybe we could learn. I actually felt Whizzy doing it: learning about me, drinking me in. Like me, Whizzy was a detective. I felt that in my chest. Ribs vibrated, shoulders buzzed with a tune that tickled between my bones. I closed my eyes to make the other senses work harder, and forgot everything in the whole world ...

Then the rain stopped and Sam came crashing down the path and – suddenly – Whizzy just wasn't there any more.

'Where did it go? I saw something like a wet firework. It can't have disappeared again! Alfie, get it back!'

The next part happened unbelievably fast. Everything was quiet now, except for the pylon – the pylon that was supposed to be dead. It was humming, and the sound was getting louder and louder. It was coming to life.

'Watch out!' somebody shrieked. 'She's electrified it!'

It was Mr Clemm.

Confused and stunned, I moved a little, but not quite quickly enough – something pulled the top of my head.

Just a few hairs, but it stung, and in the same split second, Mr Clemm took two huge strides towards us and yelled again. 'Please be careful! She can be very dangerous!'

'Alfie, quick!' Sam hissed, and he grabbed the back of my T-shirt to pull me away. I was only half breathing. More words came out of Mr Clemm's mouth – frantic words, flipped-out words – but we didn't stop to listen. We just ran.

Looking back over my shoulder was terrifying, so I only did it once, just in time to see a cable from the pylon – massively thick, like a boa constrictor – burst loose and spring into an arc that whipped the ground where we'd just been standing.

'To my house!' Sam said when we reached the gate and collected his bike. We ran, straining to hear the Bentley or Mr Clemm striding up the hill, but there were only our running feet and the *tick-tick-tick* from Sam's wheels.

'Your hair!' Sam gasped. 'It's all electrified! Are you burned?'

I slowed down and felt my scalp. My skin felt slithery and hot, but it didn't hurt. 'Nothing there.'

Sam slowed too. 'That was lucky.'

'Lucky? No, it was Mr Clemm. He saved me. I might have been electrocuted. You too! Maybe he isn't as bad as people think.'

'*What?*'

'Maybe he's weird because of the way people treat him.'

'Maybe people treat him like that because of the way he acts.' Sam sounded annoyed. 'But there's the other stuff about animals, anyway.'

'What if that isn't true? Maybe he does some scary things and some weird stuff, but he's a good bloke as well somewhere deep down.'

'So he keeps a creature like Whizzy prisoner, then when you let it out, he tries to catch it again, and suddenly you think that's fine?'

'No! 'Course I don't! But maybe we've got it wrong. Maybe he had her locked up for a good reason. And maybe he wants to catch her again to help her somehow.'

'Why have you changed your mind?' Sam was nearly shouting. 'Why have I just done you a massive favour and totally shown myself up in your street for absolutely nothing?'

'No, I'm glad you did it,' I said quickly, 'but which is the real Mr Clemm, and which is the Cloaked Strider people have terrified each other with? The people in this village have muddled Mr Clemm into a total knot.'

We were now in Sam's farmyard. He looked like I felt – soaked; beaten up T-shirt.

'Doing that stupid distraction was *so embarrassing*,' he said, 'and I've *still* missed Whizzy. What do I have to *do*?'

'I think she's shy. She needs to get to know you. If we stay close together she's bound to come back. And hey, listen – *she!* We know she's a she now! Just awesome!'

We'd almost reached Sam's front door when the weather began to change. Hot, heavy air seemed to drop down from the sky.

Sam said, 'Let's get inside.'

'Chill, we're safe here. Even if he came back, I think we could just ask him questions about her now. He knows we know her. It's all out in the open.'

But he ignored me and marched straight up to his room, which was stifling. Very quickly, everything started to feel thundery and prickly and *wrong*, but Whizzy was nowhere to be seen. There must be a thousand places to hide in a house, especially if you're faster than the wind and can drift like smoke.

17

Don't Run

Upstairs, Sam slid a game of *Covert Tour* into his Xbox.

'Sam, it's boiling in here,' I said. 'There's no way we can sit and play that.'

He kept his back to me and flicked at his controller, and a horrible feeling crept into my stomach.

'Sam?' The air up here was even heavier than outside, as if a thunder cloud had crammed into his room and was ready to crackle. 'Why don't we go out and see if Whizzy follows again? Because I've got a feeling she's somewhere close. Might be best if we get her away from the house, just in case.'

Sam didn't even look at me. His mouth was a thin mean line, and the dread in my stomach doubled.

'What if Whizzy got out of control in here and turned the electrics lethal?' I said. 'Come on, let's go outside. It can't be any hotter than it is in here.'

'What's the point? She never shows herself to me.'

'Well, it's cos I let her out,' I said. It felt funny speaking to his back. 'So she thinks I'm her rescuer ...'

He shook his head. 'She only latched on to you because you were there,' he said, tossing his controller down. It bounced and hit the wall. 'Nothing about you is special, so I don't know why you think she's yours.'

And then he muttered '*Loser*' under his breath, and I lost it and called him a loser back, and then he said it again, and the word *loser* flew around the room like an epic torpedo, and time seemed to slow down. The air felt far too close to my face and I was stuck with him in a horrible, hot cloud of crossness, just like the one at the concert.

I felt outrageous myself now. 'I'm going to look at your rabbits,' I said, 'and then I'm going home!' I spat my words, and that felt great, and blundering out of his bedroom felt good too, but he followed me, in a crashing, stomping, mad way, and somehow got ahead of me so that, suddenly, he was at the top of the stairs blocking my way.

'You're not allowed near anything on this farm without me,' he said. 'Farms are dangerous.'

'Huh! Rabbits aren't.'

'There's dangerous machinery in the rabbit barn.'

'As if I'd set that off!'

'There's the slurry tower in the yard—'

'As if I'd fall in – you have to climb a high ladder, and I'm not going to do that by accident.'

'You might do it on purpose.'

We must have been making a lot of noise because Sam's grandad appeared at the bottom of the stairs. 'Lads, lads!' he said. 'No need to blow a gasket. It's only a game.' He was holding two plates of cake and fruit. 'Snack time. Come down and take these.'

We went down. The front door was open and the smell of cut grass and summer blew inside.

'Get out in the fresh air,' his grandad said.

'Too hot,' Sam said, taking his plate.

'It's where I was going,' I said, taking mine.

His grandad laid one hand on my shoulder and the other on Sam's and shook us both gently in slow motion. 'Find some shade under a tree,' he said, 'and keep away from those silly video games.' He angled his head in the direction of Sam's room upstairs.

Sam looked up at him sharply. 'Away?'

'Yes. Away. Switch off. For your own good. You'll thank me for it one day.'

Sam asked, 'Why?'

'Why? It's just like when you lock your rabbits up for

the night, Sam. It's to protect them from foxes, but they don't know that.'

I smiled. 'Wish Mum would let me have rabbits.'

His grandad winked at me. 'They don't say a lot.'

On the way home, my luck nosedived yet again: Mr Lombard was standing at the bottom of Beggar's Hill, and the road there is too narrow for any sneakery.

'I'm watching you,' he said randomly as I passed him. 'Three strikes, my lad – three strikes and you're out!' He pointed right between my eyes. 'We don't mess about round here – we nip things in the bud.'

6.15 p.m.

I've decided that people aren't really any weirder around Whizzy. They're themselves, just *way* crosser, and it must be because of all the electricity and pressure in the air when she's around, like the feeling just before a really heavy thunderstorm breaks. The only problem with that is it means Sam *is* actually angry with me ... not as much as he seemed, but still a bit. I need to try and get Whizzy to appear properly when he's there.

There's nothing left of that atmosphere now, because it's sleeting outside. I've put a jumper on. It's July.

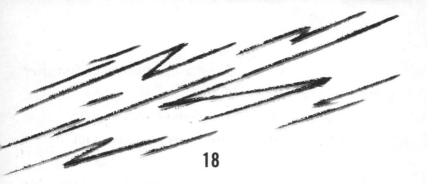

18

Escalation

Dad video-called just now. Mum spoke to him first. That worked out brilliantly, because I found out this: Mr Clemm *can't* have said anything to her about me, because I listened secretly, and she didn't tell Dad.

When it was my turn, I told him about Mr Clemm saving us from being killed by an electrical pylon tentacle, which I never would have told Mum because she'd never let me outside again. Didn't mention Whizzy. But he only wanted to talk about Lily.

'Any sign of her making friends yet?'

'Dunno,' I said. 'Why don't you ask her?'

Dad shook his head. 'You know we can't do that.'

I decided to test him. 'So what do you think about the pylon?' I asked.

'Oh?' he said. 'Haha, sounds good.'

Just as I suspected: he wasn't listening at all.

'Is Lily getting out of the house much?' Dad asked.

Lily dived on to the sofa from nowhere. 'Dad, are you serious? Don't pick on me and *my* stuff all the time,' she said. 'Did you hear any of what he just said? He told you a bunch of crazy lies about weird old men saving him from electrical octopus tentacles to cover up some bad thing he's done, and you didn't even notice!' She was definitely not meant to hear all that stuff. At least she thought I was lying. She pointed to me. 'Alfie does stuff and gets away with it the *whole time*.'

'I do *not*.'

'OK, that's enough,' Dad said. 'Lily, sit down with me. Talk to me.'

She's still having her turn now. In fact, she's talking to Dad but not concentrating on him properly, because she keeps looking at me strangely. I definitely should have been more careful.

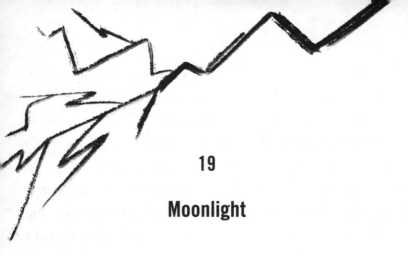

19

Moonlight

30th July, 2.30 a.m.

Woke at 2 a.m. – couldn't get back to sleep. Came back from the loo and saw a light under Lily's door. An abnormal light, like part of the moon had got into her room. Her door wasn't completely closed, so I slid inside and saw one of the most unforgettable sights of this whole adventure so far: Whizzy floating. Whizzy rippling in slow, graceful oblong shapes right above Lily's bed as she slept.

It was beautiful. Whizzy was the colour of moonlight and as gentle as a rainbow.

Whizzy wasn't as big as she can get, either. She was the same size as the length of Lily's bed. This was a different, careful Whizzy. Doing Lily good, almost nursing her – that's what it looked like. Maybe Whizzy's trying to make up for almost hurting her after the concert. Or maybe Whizzy just knows when people need mending.

But still, it was scary. *She can be very dangerous*, Mr Clemm said. How could I know what was really happening?

I wondered how a photo might come out. Something to show Sam. Moving more slowly and carefully than ever in my life, I crept back to my bedroom for my phone, zoomed the camera in on Whizzy, clicked … and she vanished.

The photo didn't catch her. There's just Lily's bedroom wall.

9.30 a.m.

At breakfast just now, Lily demanded an egg. Mum's face stayed straight and set, but her eyes looked excited; Lily hasn't been able to keep much down at breakfast for two years. It's her worst time. And now she wants eggs. Mum struggled so much to pretend to be casual that I felt quite sorry for her. Then Lily went out and I heard Mum telling Dad on the phone. 'I hardly dare believe it, Jerome,' she said. 'She's eating eggs and potatoes again … I know! Two years at least. And her face is filling out. It's like a dream come true.'

I bit my nails all through that. What if something goes wrong? Whizzy's a wild creature. Anything might happen. It still feels weird even having Lily home from hospital, so … what if Whizzy makes a mistake?

Time to go out again. Sam's waiting, and today's the day he's going to see Whizzy. I'm determined.

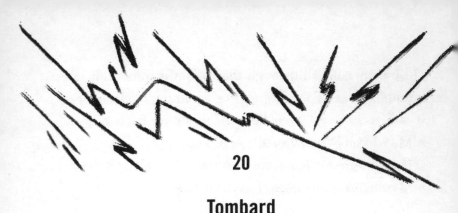

20

Tombard

<u>3.30 p.m.</u>

Typing this in my bedroom, but can't stay here. Need to get back to Lilac Farm, but Mum won't let me. She says they won't want me there.

And now there's a text from Dad:

Dad: *How today?*

Will he even notice if I tell him? Is there any point?

Me: *Disaster. Sam thinks it's my fault, and it is, but didn't mean it*
Dad: *Fallen out? It'll blow over. What happened?*

I had to stop and think. We aren't supposed to tell Dad anything worrying when he's miles away.

Me: *Some lads. Doesn't matter*
Dad: *Alfie? What's happened?*
Me: *Just some stupid stuff with lads. We're all OK*

It started out so brilliantly. The plan was to lure Whizzy down so Sam could see her. We met on the rec field. We weren't quite sure how we'd do it, but it had to involve electricity. We both wore our football shirts because they make epic amounts of static, and rubbed them against our bellies again and again. Couldn't wait for him to see her properly.

Sam's hair was just starting to stand on end with the static when this bunch of lads appeared. The tallest of the group had pale hair, and eyebrows so white they were hardly there.

I nudged Sam. 'Who's that?'

'Tombard.' His voice was low and full of a million warnings. 'He's in Year Nine. Lives in Newton Moorby.'

'Tom Bard?

'Thomas Lombard. But always called Tombard – never Thomas.'

'Why?'

'Dunno. Too many Toms in his class, probably. You know what it's like for Toms in ours. But you don't get it wrong. Not with him. Mr Lombard is his grandad.'

I shuddered and pulled a face. 'Who are the others?'

'They're his gang. You don't get too near them. No one does.'

They had an excellent premiership ball, and the four of them started kicking it around us.

'Wanna go?' said the short one.

Sam didn't answer. The ball rolled towards us. I felt all zappy and full of skills, so I dribbled it across the field. The short one tackled it off me, but I won it back. He did a step-over and I kicked it away from him before he could cross it.

'*Don't,*' Sam hissed, very low and quiet.

'It's OK – we can just have a kick-about,' I whispered. And then Tombard said, 'To me!' And we worked out goals and teams without hardly saying a word. Sam hung back to start with, then scored a revolutionary goal. I scissor-kicked a lustrous one in.

Tombard saluted me. 'Gifted, man! Skillage in the village!'

His voice buzzed through my shoes, up into my feet, and hit my knees like electricity. Whizzy? But there wasn't time to think. The ball came back my way.

It felt like the game went on for hours. It was beautiful. I did moves I'd never even dreamed of, and Sam was untouchable. It was pure Whizzy magic making us ourselves but way better, and it was brilliant because there was no way Sam could ever doubt her now.

'See?' I said. 'She's making us supreme! She's a talent-magnifying streak of brilliance!'

Sam nodded and grinned. His whole face had come to life. This couldn't have been more perfect.

Suddenly, Whizzy zoomed out of a bush and went fizzing over to a nearby bench. I nudged Sam and tried to point her out with careful signals so that the gang wouldn't see, but by that time, she was underneath it and out of sight. She'd looked all excited.

'He isn't as bad as he usually is at school,' Sam whispered. 'Do you really think it's her doing it?'

A tour around the village was mentioned, and without anyone asking us, Sam and I were on it. Tombard isn't the kind of person you disagree with, Sam had said. If someone looks like they might be about to, they get a stare, and the idea dies in the air.

The tour started at the river, but not for stone skimming. The river was attacked. There was kick splashing, boulder smashing, pushing – everything. The wild flat-out craziness of it was mega exciting. Even Sam was infected.

'Look!' Sam grabbed my arm as we scrambled back to the road. 'That's her, isn't it?' The telephone wires above our heads were steaming. 'Yah. I think she loves this – looks like she's playing too.'

I nodded. Sam finally getting to see her in action was just the coolest thing *ever*. And soon, she'd lose her shyness and trust him enough to appear fully – for *sure*.

It was my idea to go up the hill. I was trying to keep us as far from Ash House as possible, just in case, because otherwise, why wouldn't a tour end up at the weirdest and most interesting place of all?

'Let's go up the hill and get cooler,' I said. It was almost lunchtime by now, and roasting. Waves of heat rolled along the road. 'The higher you go, the cooler it gets.'

'Let's not,' Sam murmured to me.

'It'll be fine,' I said. 'It'll be fun.' Maybe Whizzy was making me more *me*, too.

'Up to his house?' asked Tombard, nodding at Sam.

'No,' Sam said quickly, blinking a lot. 'Too many of us.'

'Where then?'

'Just up. Just higher,' I said.

Sam shot looks at me. He was trying to say no without actually saying the word, but Tombard nodded and away we went.

I know all their names now. The big one is Matthew, the short one is Noel, and then there's Kiran – another brown person besides me, yay!

'Last one to Beggar's Lane's a piece of sewer grease!' Tombard shouted, shoving Sam into Kiran. Seconds later, everyone was running up the hill with Tombard and Noel in the lead, Sam and Kiran next, and me and Matthew close behind, starting to overtake. Tombard screamed at the top of his voice like a mad witch, making us laugh till we went all weak. Then he swerved into Beggar's Lane and we tore down the steep little drop with the breeze in our faces, dipping like seals, legs pumping automatically – we were nearly flying.

It was supernatural. Dizzying. The giddiness was like nothing I've ever known, like a giant was blowing bubbles and we were fizzing right at the top of them, laughing instead of breathing.

Still cackling, Tombard turned the corner into Brackenbury Row and spilt into the allotments, legs splayed, out of control. Sam skidded to a halt. All the wildness left me and an uneasy feeling crept in. The air was virtually crackling with Whizzy's power.

Sam's told me about the allotments. It looks like a jumble of sheds and greenhouses and vegetable patches, but it's him and his grandad's special place.

'Not here,' Sam said, panting, and looking as hot as I felt. 'My grandad might be here.'

The gang came to a juddering, gasping standstill, all of us even hotter and sweatier now we'd stopped running.

Tombard looked straight at Sam. 'So?'

'So we can't,' Sam said.

The others watched. Tombard let a little silence hang for a few seconds, then he said, 'Can't what?'

'We can't mess about,' Sam said. 'Not in here.'

'Who can't?'

Matthew kicked the ground impatiently and blew air out of his mouth in fast spurts.

'*Who* can't?' Tombard repeated.

My stomach clenched. I swallowed, trying to keep my eyes away from Whizzy, who was very small – practically invisible – just a blood-red glint on a branch. Hadn't seen her turn that colour before. Couldn't help looking again, and she was growing. Her blood-red insides shimmered and pulsed, like something was overheating and going out of control. There was a rhythm to it, like an engine inside her was going *Womp WOMP WOMP!* Was she reacting to Tombard's awful vibe?

We should have turned and cleared out of there right then. I should have grabbed Sam and *just run*. Why didn't I?

The gang moved forward. So did I. So did Sam. Matthew swaggered in and out of the vegetable patches doing rap moves.

Blackbirds tweeted warning calls. Mown grass and nettle smells filled the air and we kept going, past greenhouses and cold frames and things that none of us recognised except Sam. The cool breeze we'd had on the hill was gone, and even my breath felt hot.

'Doesn't matter,' I said, because now, Noel and Matthew were wrestling each other to the ground.

'Ah ... you're strangling me, man!' one of them squawked, and they rolled into a vegetable patch.

Tombard yanked some curly green vegetables out of the ground and scattered them, breaking the neat rows. Everyone laughed. Everyone except me and Sam.

Tombard pulled some onions out next and kicked them across the allotment like mini footballs.

'Wu-hoo, you're on fire!' Kiran said, and shot a load of spit at a bush, like some kind of lizard. They were still giddy. Sam and I were definitely not. Tombard scooted to the back of one of the sheds and came out carrying a long-handled tool.

When he started to bash through the vegetables with the wiry metal end, churning up clods of earth and chopped-up leaves and stalks, Sam hissed to me, 'What's he doing? Has Whizzy's stuff got into him?'

I tried to explain that it wasn't really *stuff*. 'It's just her weather side effects, like in the hall the other night. It makes people more … full-on. Magnified.'

Sam looked completely horrified. 'Tombard? *More* extreme? Can't you stop it?'

'Um, yeah, I—'

'Can't you get her to burst a cloud over them? Make a storm when we need one, for once?' His hands were in fists.

The others were looking at Tombard like he'd gone mad, but then they joined in.

Tombard carried on tearing up the curly vegetables and Kiran found a garden fork, and soon the whole patch was a mass of soil and broken plants. White goo came out of the split stems. It looked exactly like school glue. Some of the prongs fell out of Tombard's tool and lay on the ground, curling like claws in the middle of the mess. A smell of onions hit my nostrils and this morning's football game seemed like something nice that had happened to me a long time ago.

'Epic!' Matthew said. Noel looked a bit scared, but you could see that they'd do anything as long as Tombard didn't laugh at them.

'Alfie, you have to make her stop,' Sam muttered, without taking his eyes off Tombard's movements.

I just stared at him like I'd been frozen to the spot, and I think I had. The dread in my stomach was spreading through my veins and I felt sick, shaky, useless.

'Get her to come out and show herself – that'll make them stop!' he said.

'No! It'll be fine.' I tried to pull myself together. 'Like at the concert, she gets better if you just think happy thoughts. We have to try – concentrate ...'

Sam stared at the wreckage with wild eyes. 'It'll be fine? *How?*'

'It's not her fault!' I hissed. 'She doesn't understand enough. Not yet. She will one day soon ...'

'She's getting worse,' Sam said.

'She's getting stronger ...'

Then Sam turned to look at something, so I turned too, and saw his grandad striding slowly towards us.

Too late to run or hide. Too late to do anything.

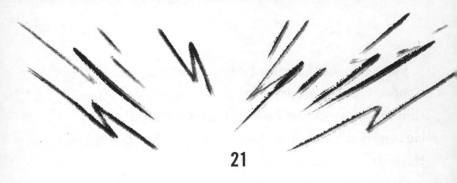

21

Grandad

'Hey! What are you doing there? Stop! Sam! What do you think you're doing?'

Sam's grandad's shadow fell over the ruined vegetables, and Sam looked down then up again at his grandad's face as if he didn't recognise it.

'Nothing,' Sam said. 'I'm not doing anything.'

My heart thumped madly. My forehead was covered with sweat.

His grandad took a step closer. Tombard did not step back.

Sam said, 'It's OK, Grandad – it's nothing – it's OK.' I could hear panic bubbling in his throat.

'It isn't nothing. This is George Manley's patch.'

Sam's grandad turned to Tombard and shouted, 'Put that down!' But Tombard didn't even look at him. He wasn't bothered.

Sam's grandad took another step. 'Good grief, lad! Let go of it – it isn't yours.'

Tombard stuck the tool in the ground but didn't let go. He stared at Sam's grandad. Sam stood still, looking as if he might cry, and then his grandad bent and grabbed the tool near its wiry end and the tug of war began.

I could hear their breath. Tombard's came down his nose and was short and fast; Sam's grandad's came out of his mouth in loud gasps. Then Tombard did let go. A great big lump of horror settled in my chest as the handle swung back and hit Sam's grandad in the chest, and he bent backwards and toppled … but he didn't fall. He was winded and gasping, but still held the tool.

The gang ran off without saying a word, and disappeared through the bottom gate.

'Grandad!' Sam said, but his grandad just looked at him. Such a look. I'd have hated it if my dad – anyone – had looked at me like that. As if he didn't even *like* Sam. Neither of them spoke.

I wanted to melt into the ground so I didn't have to see their faces any longer, but then it ended, because Sam set off running.

I said, 'S-sorry, Mr Irwin,' and plunged after Sam, skidding across the allotments, desperate to keep him in sight.

I could tell he didn't know where he was going. He ran down the other side of Brackenbury Row towards the woods, and at first, I could see him really clearly, even though he was well in front of me – he's a brilliant runner – but then I lost him. That big house by the bridge did it. He must have darted away somewhere down there.

I bawled at the top of my lungs, 'SAM!'

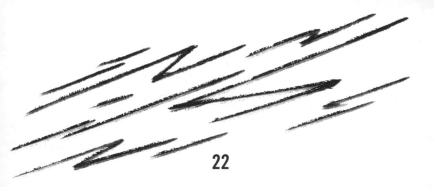

22

Lilac Farm

The road smelt rubbery hot, like something was cooking. Going home seemed like the only thing to do, but the further I went, the worse things felt. The village seemed full of windows, shining like eyes that had seen everything I'd ever done.

So I turned round. There was so much to fix, and I had to start with Sam, so I forced my slack legs to do it all again. To trek all the way back to the terrible vegetable patch – but nobody was there. The patch had been raked over. Most of the slashed plants had been pulled up and were now sitting in a weird little pile on the grass. His grandad must have done that. The wiry tool had disappeared and so had Kiran's fork. I ran behind the shed and there they were, leaning up against the wooden wall where his grandad must have put them, and there was Sam too, crouching, head down. Sort of crumpled.

He knew I was there – he got into a straighter position – but he didn't look up. His eyes and lips were puffy and he sniffed every few seconds. A bluebottle had got inside the shed and was battering itself against the window, making bumps.

The bumps got to me, and I blurted, 'Where's your grandad?'

Sam shrugged, but kept his eyes down.

'Did you help mend the patch?'

He shook his head.

'Thought you'd gone home,' I said, and my tongue felt too big for my mouth.

He didn't answer. A bird sang somewhere high above, all alone.

'Sam. Go home.'

He turned to me. He looked like he wanted to kill me.

'I'll come with you if you want.' I felt like crying too. 'I can tell him what happened. How Tombard makes everyone do stuff.'

He stood and walked away without looking at me again. I didn't know what to do, so I followed him, sick bubbles coming up from my churning stomach. He went out of the allotment and turned up Beggar's Hill. I trailed after him, staying silent. He didn't look back, but he knew I was there.

Didn't think we'd ever get to Lilac Farm, but when we did, his grandad's car was in the drive.

Inside, apart from our breathing, the house was quiet. In the kitchen, the fridge shuddered. Sam opened it and poured himself a drink of orange juice. The smell of the allotments was still hanging in my nose: a cabbagey smell with roses in it.

'When we find your grandad,' I said, 'I'll tell him it was my idea to go with them, and that you didn't want to.' I had to fill this silence, so went rabbiting on. 'I should have said that straight away, but listen, if I explain it all now, it'll be OK …'

Sam snorted. 'It's always OK for you, isn't it?' he said, walking between the fridge and the table, then back to the fridge. 'But it's always you. It's everything you do.'

'What d'you mean?'

'It's always your idea and it's always going to be fine, but it never is for anyone but you.'

My stomach felt as if the kitchen was tilting. 'I didn't mean for this to happen …'

'Not just today. You never wait and you never ask. You just plunge ahead, and you always come out of it OK. Nothing sticks to you – except the good bits. You get to meet Whizzy, and I get all the trouble. And I'm sick of it.'

I didn't know what to do, but thought I'd better let him say it all. But when he'd finished and both of us were just standing there, the stillness in the house felt really strange, as if something had gone even more wrong.

'Where's your mum and Roan?'

He ignored me, went to the bottom of the stairs and roared, 'GRANDAD!'

No answer. He went to the back door, which was already open.

'Grandad!' he screamed again. He waited for a moment, then looked at me. I bit my lip.

And then we shouted together, 'GRANDAD!'

We shouted it in the sitting room, up the stairs and in the garden.

He was in the greenhouse. He'd been watering the tomato plants – except he wasn't watering any more. He was lying down.

There was mess all around him: soil from knocked-over plants and water in a pool from the running hose, turning the soil to mud.

Sam crouched. 'Grandad,' he whispered, and put a hand on his grandad's shoulder, but the only thing moving was his chest. He was on his side, his hair and one cheek flat against the greenhouse floor. I phoned Mum so that she could order an ambulance properly and come and help.

'Grandad,' Sam said again, but there was only silence.

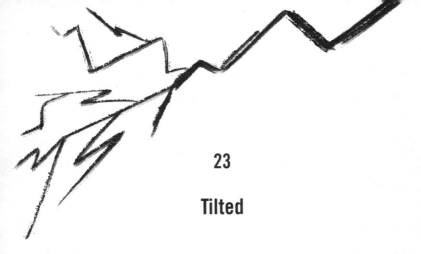

23

Tilted

Everyone arrived at once. Sam's mum with Roan, my mum, and seconds after that, the ambulance.

Everything got organised quickly, and both our cars followed the ambulance down Beggar's Hill as if the ambulance was pulling us.

Mum just phoned Sam's mum at the hospital and found out what happened.

'It was a stroke,' Mum told me. 'His grandad's lost his speech.'

Her voice sounded too loud. 'How can it be lost?' I asked.

'The stroke has taken his voice and paralysed his left side, Alfie,' she said. 'Strokes often do that.'

'What's a stroke?'

'It's something that's happened to Mr Irwin's brain,' she said, too carefully. 'A blood vessel's burst or a clot has formed. It's interfered with the blood supply to that part of his brain.'

Blood. I couldn't look at her. I wanted to talk through my fingers. 'How long will it last?'

Mum glided over to me and stroked my back in little circles. 'They don't know. He's very poorly, sweetheart. But it's a blessing Sam was there, and you with him.'

This felt like being underwater. Things were muffled. Other things were numb, and my feet felt miles away. 'Can't he say anything at all?'

'Not really,' Mum said. 'Not properly. The words won't form.'

4.25 p.m.

I've come upstairs. Lily followed me when I first came up, and just stood in my bedroom doorway.

'Can't talk about it,' I said.

She bit her lip, hovered for a second not looking at anything, then went back downstairs.

I still feel shaky. The destruction, Tombard … Everything's going round and round in my head, but it all comes down to one thing: Whizzy. Sam's right. She doesn't mean to be, but she's totally out of control, and all because I let her out. That's what I can't tell Mum and Lily.

_6.45 p.m._

Wanted to ring Sam just now, but Mum won't let me. They're not even back from hospital yet.

'Let me text Cindy again and see how Sam's doing first,' she said, so she did, and that's how I found out he doesn't want to see me when they get home.

'Look,' Mum said, 'it's only natural. Give him a couple of days and I'm sure he'll be fine. He just needs to be by himself. It doesn't mean he hates you.'

But I know he does.

2nd August, 1.45 p.m.

Mum and Lily keep nosing their heads round the door. Sometimes it's to see what I want to eat next. (The answer has only been this: banana sandwiches and crisp sandwiches.)

Often, it's just, 'Are you OK?' (And there's no answer to that.)

The whole village found out what happened within seconds. Mum says villages are like that. She also keeps giving me the 'peer-pressure resistance' talk. 'Walk away next time, Alfie.' She's said this about a hundred times. 'Walk away faster!'

She can't figure out how I fell into it. 'You've got such a strong temperament,' she said, shaking her head. But she hasn't met Tombard.

I think Lily understands. She hasn't said much, but when I first came home and spilt out the whole story, she shook her head and bit her lip and looked like she was remembering things from her old school.

They just carried Dad up to my room on Mum's laptop. Tried to tell him how everything's been, but my words fell out in a muddle, ending with, '… and Sam still hates me.'

'Chin up,' Dad said. 'You'll be back playing footie again before you know it. Make the most of your free time and get outside training. Lily's been out a lot, Mum says. You need to do the same. No point sulking in your room.'

'I'm not.'

'Lily says you've hardly been anywhere.'

'Been out today. It was appalling.'

'Oh, Alfie, it can't have been that bad.'

'It was. We had to go to Lily's doctor appointment, and Mum got talking to the mum of a small guy in the year below me, and he made cutthroat signals to Lily behind his mum's back – the whole time. About me. Definitely about me.'

'It might not have been …'

'Was. Could tell by the way he shook his head and pretended to back away from me slowly, as if I might do something. And even worse – Mr Lombard came up to me in the street afterwards and accused *me* of leading *Tombard* astray!'

He said this was Strike Two. He didn't say what Strike One was, but I'd guess it was trespassing. Didn't tell Dad that part. How am I ever going to leave this house again? Whizzy'll act up as soon as I do – I just know it.

'It'll all blow over soon.'

'Lily actually defended me, for only the second time in history. She called him a loser, using hand signals, then said, "Just because he was there, doesn't mean he did it."'

'Well that was—'

'Then she called him a daddy-shortlegs, and Mum exploded. There was nearly an incident.'

Dad laughed.

'Couldn't you come home and make some steel in England for a bit?'

'Alfie, I'd love to, but you know how things are.'

'Can we come to Sweden?'

'No. Too expensive. We need to rebuild after last year.'

'How come you've taught Lily some Swedish and not me?'

'Ah, Lily's been at it, has she?'

'She called me a *dumma fåne* and wouldn't tell me what it meant. I had to go online. Why did you teach her to call me a stupid fool?'

'I didn't. She asked me for a Swedish insult – it wasn't meant for you. But she's got her sense of humour back, which is fantastic!'

And then it was *Lily, Lily, Lily* again, and I might as well not have been there.

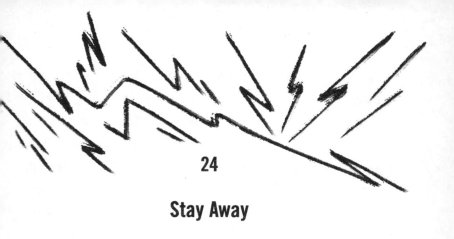

24

Stay Away

5th August

Stories are *still* going round the village. They're saying I whacked Sam's grandad round the head with a massive stick and that's why he's in hospital.

When I told Mum, she pulled me on to her knee (which I don't in any way fit on any more). 'A lie is halfway round the world before the truth has got its boots on,' she said gently.

I smiled. I nearly laughed. 'How can I fix it?'

'By putting out better stories. Stories about the good things you've done. What happened wasn't really your fault in that you didn't *do* the vandalism, but you were *with* the vandals. You have to be *seen* to be making amends. Do you see that?'

I kind of did, but …

'So you can help one of my ladies.'

'Help? How?'

Mum's a care coordinator. She sits in the town hall and (either over the phone or online) makes sure elderly people get meals and any help at home when they need it.

'Pick up Mrs Gillespie's groceries from the shop,' Mum said. 'The list will already be made up. Then take it round to her at the old people's bungalows. Number three. You can do something like that every other day from now on.'

'Wait … Do I have to cook it for her?'

'No, Alfie! But you might have to put her shopping away.'

'Who will care about that? Who will even know?'

'Everyone will know, Alfie! Look how quickly word got round about your mishap! Mrs Gillespie will care, and it's the right thing to do.'

_12.30 p.m._

Not sure Mum's plan will work. The only person who needs to see me doing good deeds is Mr Lombard, and it'll take a lot more than fixing old people's shopping for him to change his mind about me. Sam won't care. The morning's gone and he still hasn't turned up or messaged me. I've texted SORRY a hundred times. Well, perhaps about thirty times.

Back from my mission, which was more helpful, less helpful, and a million times stranger than I expected. (Typing like mad now – had to wrestle Lily for the laptop, and she'll be back for it soon.)

The old people's bungalows are at the top of the other hill in the village, called Raven's Rise, which is a lot smaller than Beggar's Hill, and on the opposite side of the valley.

Mrs Gillespie has a footprint embedded in her doorstep – someone must have stepped on the concrete before it dried – and I was laughing at that when she answered the door, which is why she said, 'Ooh – it's Dina's boy! Alfie Bradley! Such a nice smiley face to brighten up the afternoon. And what a huge bag of shopping to lug around. That's it, leave the front door open – it's so hot. Come in, my angel – come in.'

I stared. My mouth probably fell open and everything, because Mrs Gillespie is the old lady who was arguing with Mr Lombard in the village hall! Mr Clemm's friend with the silver-beaded hair! At first, I felt a bit better, like everything was coming back together again. Mrs Gillespie is the same colour as my African-American grandad, the one I never met, and her accent is all rounded and fruity and not from round here.

And straight away, just like she'd been kind to Mr Clemm at the jumble sale, she made me feel snuggled and safe. She called me things like 'my eaglet', and hobbled around her house without her stick, using her furniture like a walking frame.

The air inside hung hot and heavy, but Mrs Gillespie smelt of flowers. 'Now then, I've been baking ginger snaps today – how's that for a stroke of luck? Put the shopping on the kitchen table, would you, my pet? Milk and cold things in the fridge. Tins in the tin cupboard. You'll find it.'

In the kitchen, the back door was open and a breeze blew in. And as I started unpacking, Whizzy blew in too. Out of the corner of my eye, I saw a line of crazy white light zip through the door and up to the ceiling, and immediately the lightbulb started to fizz.

I felt as if a trap was closing.

Mrs Gillespie was still in her front room and sitting in a chair that faced away from the kitchen. She hadn't noticed a thing. My heart started thumping. Going out had been a terrible idea. Helping had been a terrible idea. I needed to get out of there fast and take Whizzy with me, so I just carried on putting stuff away at top speed while a perfect letter Z formed out of white light above my head. Didn't take my eyes off it. Felt for space in the fridge for the milk and butter. The light straightened out, then zipped into a backwards letter *Z*, like Whizzy was showing off.

The letter *Z* got faster and more frantic. The lightbulb turned smoky grey. There was a burning smell and I started to panic … What if there was a fire? (You can't put water on an electrical fire … can you? I need to know these things. I need to get better training, and fast.) And poor Mrs Gillespie still sat there with her back to all of it.

'Please don't, Whizzy,' I whispered. 'Not here.'

Poor Whizzy. It must be scary and a bit sad to almost set fire to something everywhere you go.

Back in the front room, Mrs Gillespie held out a plateful of golden-brown twigs that smelt of syrupy ginger. I took one and she shrugged her shoulders and grinned, showing white, even teeth that looked too good to be true.

Whizzy was closer. The air flowed into the room differently, and I smelt rubbery warmth and hot coins. A clock on the wall ticked loud and slow, far louder than the faint sizzling sound coming from Whizzy's antics.

'Here, take another couple and sit down, Alfie,' she said. 'Make yourself comfy in that easy chair.' Her eyes glittered with granny-ness. It felt like being in a bedtime story.

'I've got to go, Mrs Gillespie.'

'Oh, so soon?'

Mrs Gillespie still had her back to the kitchen, but

Whizzy hadn't finished with that lightbulb. Light shot from it in blades of a strange green, which turned to dark red, like a coal fire. (*How* does Whizzy do that?)

'You'll come again, won't you, Alfie?'

'OK, Mrs Gillespie.'

I was almost at the front door. The lightbulb was now the darkest, blackest shade of red ever. It fizzed one final time, then sputtered out like a dying firework.

'And call me Cleona. Sweet spider-leg eyelashes you have,' she said, chuckling, and I tried to join in, but stopped when I saw what was happening to the kitchen ceiling. The area around the bulb was blackening. Smoke, much thicker than before, was rippling out in yellowy-grey waves that blew into the lounge and out of the front door. I had to do something.

Mrs Gillespie began to cough and, turning to look at her crazy, toxic kitchen, tried to stand up, failed, and I dived across the floor shouting, 'No! Stop! Please!' at Whizzy, and the next few minutes were chaos, with Mrs Gillespie shrieking, and me trying to calm her down, and Mrs Gillespie starting to call 999, then stopping when she realised the smoke had all blown away. The ceiling was blackened, the floor was a sooty, gungy mess, and the lightbulb was in pieces, but it was all now as cold as an extinct volcano.

'The electricity people,' I said. 'That's who you need to phone. Your wiring's all melted.'

She nodded. Her mouth looked all tucked in and puckered with worry. 'But whatever can have happened? Oh, Alfie, what a good job you were here to spot that.'

I felt myself heating up. It was all my fault just for visiting. I was nodding and smiling dumbly when my breath stopped: Mr Clemm was striding up Mrs Gillespie's path, carrying the picnic box.

Before I could pull myself together even a tiny bit, the front door was opening and Mrs Gillespie was saying, 'My, my! Look at you all spruced up! Suits you. Keep it up!' and Mr Clemm was inside and gigantic and unreal.

'Come and see what's been happening in here, Nathaniel,' Mrs Gillespie said. 'This young man is a hero.' She linked her arm through his and they set off to the kitchen together like a lopsided daddy-long-legs.

'Alfie Bradley,' he said to me as they passed. Just that. His forehead gleamed with sweat. How could someone so terrifying ever be a good guy? Didn't trust myself to speak, so held up my hand in a strange waving greeting. Inside, I quaked.

I followed them into the kitchen, where Mr Clemm put the picnic box on the table and opened the lid. A smell of birds clung to him.

Suddenly I knew what needed to happen, but it felt like

the most awful thing I'd ever had to do in my life. Nothing else could possibly get Whizzy under control, but … it was terrifying. What might he do to her? Could I really risk it?

'Erm, Mr Clemm,' I said, 'I need to ask you something.' My heart battered my chest, but the words were out.

He looked at me. 'Is it to do with our speedy friend?'

I nodded. 'Things are getting out of control.'

'Yes,' he said, glancing from the ceiling to the floor. 'Yes, I think they are. Come to the house.'

The next ten minutes was a jumble of me and Mr Clemm not telling Mrs Gillespie what had really happened and making sure she'd got a definite time for an electrician to call (Mr Clemm did that) and cleaning up the black-and-red mess from her kitchen floor (I did that, with a dustpan and brush. It was weird wet soot, almost like syrup. Or lava).

Mr Clemm was so busy making sure Mrs Gillespie was OK that when I said I had to go home, neither of them really noticed. But when I got to the top of Raven's Rise, I looked back over my shoulder. Mrs Gillespie was standing in the doorway, watching me go.

Then a voice, gruff and cross, came from the bottom of the hill – 'You again! What's happening up there?' – and Mr Lombard huffed across the road. 'Don't forget – three strikes and you're out!'

I shrugged and tried to head for home, but he stopped walking and fixed his eyes on me as I passed. (He *still* looked like he had a cold, so maybe he didn't have one. Maybe that watery soreness is just his look.)

'Cleona?' he shouted. 'Cleona? Is that smoke? What's going on? Trouble and this lad are never far apart.'

My head pounded as much as if he'd screamed it in my face. Walking on was horrible, but down the other side of the rise a deep purple zigzag flashed in front of me, really close, like a piece of dark lightning, and I nearly fell off the kerb.

I knew exactly who it was. Squeezing my eyes tight shut, I shouted at her, 'GO AWAY!'

Even before I opened my eyes, I felt bad about it. And when I did open them, Whizzy had gone, and Tombard was hoofing it up the road towards me.

'Yo,' he barked. 'Talking to yourself now? Freaky!'

He must have been looking for his grandad. Didn't give him time to say more. I just ran.

6.05 p.m.

Made a few drawings of Whizzy, but none of them are any good.

Phoned Sam, but he won't pick up.

Just had a nightmare. I was trapped upstairs in Ash House inches from a moth with no mouth, which was crawling towards my face and I couldn't move. Mr Lombard's footsteps were coming up the stairs – he was seconds away from finding me – and Sam was laughing at home in his bedroom.

Then it turned into Whizzy making it rain more than it's ever rained before, and the whole village was swept away in a flash flood. Then when everyone was rescued, just when they'd finished drying their houses out, she made everything freeze so hard the whole village cracked and shattered, even the people. And it was all my fault.

No way am I going to Ash House. Too scary. Not worth it. Completely sure, now, that I'm just going to stay indoors forever. Mr Clemm can sort this whole thing out. Nothing good happens when me and Whizzy hit this village.

9th August, 10.15 a.m.

I have to go to Ash House. I just don't know what else to do. I'm too tangled in this whole mess now, and I have to make sure Mr Clemm helps, because this just happened:

Lily came into my room and said, 'It's raining, but only

on our house.' She stood there staring, like she was waiting for me to do something about it.

Outside, the rain's coming down in thin, slanting needles. It starts at the edge of our front garden and stops at the edge of our back garden. Sideways, it stops around the part where our roof joins on to next door, and just now I could hear them opening and closing doors, shouting to each other to come and look.

There's no other sign of Whizzy. The air smells of flowers and leaves, not burning rubber. I think she's apologising.

The raincloud is quite close to our roof, and there's no other cloud in the sky. At any other time, it would have been fabulous, but Usher's Place is filling up with people. Our house is getting famous, and not in a good way. Feels like this whole thing could flip over into a total runaway mess.

I suddenly realised Lily was still looking at me. 'I don't know how you've done this,' she said, 'but I know it was something to do with you. Get it sorted.'

_2.30 p.m._

I'm back, but everything's changed. It went like this:

Telling Mum I needed to go to Ash House was cringe city. I knew she'd ask why, and I'd practised the answer till I was perfectly slick, but she didn't swallow it:

'Because he's got this strange creature. It's very fast, but comes and goes and needs careful handling. He needs help to get it properly back and under control, and I'm good at dealing with it.'

'Something about that sounds very unlikely, Alfie. What are you really doing up there? And does he even know you're coming? And in any case, I'm not about to let you loose on the property of that peculiar man. He was quite nice with it, but … no.' She shuddered.

'It's all fine – I'll be safe. I—'

'What's the animal? Is it dangerous? And why you?'

Then Lily stepped in. 'Oh, I think you should let him go, Mum. It'll do him good to have a job.'

I blinked at Lily in a total daze. *What was she doing?*

Mum still looked suspicious. 'We don't know enough about this man. I've only met him once.'

'Well why don't we all go, then?' Lily said. 'Problem solved! And I get to see Julia the cat again! I told you about her hair falling out, didn't I, Mum?'

I looked for an evil glint in her eye, but there wasn't one. She genuinely wanted to help … but it was a horrific idea. How would Mr Clemm be able to say anything with Mum and Lily listening?

On the way there, the two of them talked about how strange it would be to meet Mr Clemm properly and how unusual he sounded when he spoke.

'I noticed it the other week,' Mum said. 'He enunciates the final syllable of every word very firmly. I can't remember hearing anybody speak in quite that way.'

I didn't reply. I was too busy telling myself I wasn't going to be fatally embarrassed, over and over again.

'Alfie,' Mum said, 'why are you muttering?'

Halfway Lane was having a hot summer's day. When we got to Mr Clemm's door, the full horror of this whole mangled plan hit me in the stomach. Breathing in big gulps of air helped, but when Mum pressed the strange old-fashioned crab-shaped doorbell, the panic rose right up into my mouth.

Mum's eyes were out on stalks at the fossilised metal graveyard surrounding us, but when the door opened, we all spoke at once.

I said, 'Sorry, but we've all come ...' at the same time as Mum said, 'I hope we're not intruding ...' and Lily said, 'Hello, Mr Clemm!'

My heart was beating fast. I'm sure my lips twitched.

Mr Clemm just stood there smiling in a very tall way.

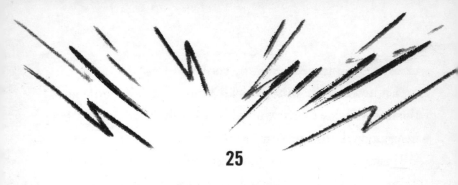

25

The Giant's House

Inside, things were dark and crammed. Old furniture. Messy books and papers. Instruments on the walls – a barometer, a compass, and things I didn't recognise that looked like they belonged on a ship. The smell was fusty: coal fires, ink, dusty old carpets … and horses. I'd imagined this house. I'd dreamed it, and now we were here.

He led us to the kitchen at the back and when we got there, a long, horrible silence took over. Mr Clemm swayed backwards and forwards on his huge legs and seemed to have no more idea of what to say than I did. Mum started small talk about the weather, which broke Mr Clemm's awkwardness a bit. He buried himself in making a big pot of tea and looked at Mum sideways a couple of times. He didn't meet my eyes at all.

Nobody sat down, because we hadn't been told to.

Nobody except Julia, that is. She was sitting tall on a kitchen chair, as if waiting for her dinner. Everything ordinary was right next to everything strange: table, chairs, hairless cat. Kettle, teapot, gigantic man with contraptions and mini-zoo.

Then Mum got specific and my heart sank further. 'Alfie tells me you need him to help you with a beast!'

Mr Clemm looked flustered.

'Is it dangerous?' asked Mum bluntly. 'What is it?'

'Well,' Mr Clemm hid his face by rummaging for teaspoons. 'It's a … It's hard to say. It's very … unusual.'

'Is it a big creature?'

'Well, it rather depends …' Mr Clemm opened his arms wide and looked from one hand to the other, but he probably shouldn't have, because his outstretched arms just looked absolutely *ginormous*, and Mum frowned. Lily and I locked eyes.

Then, unbelievably, Lily came to the rescue. She did it in classic Lily smooth-and-innocent style. 'Mr Clemm,' she said, 'do you think I could see the animals?'

Short, neat, and the way she said *I* and not *we* was genius. Mum could either stay and make more awkward talk, or look after Lily. I was grateful – my head frothed with it – but at the same time, I felt like ducking. This was Lily. There had to be a catch.

'Do you like birds?' Mr Clemm asked. Lily nodded. 'Then meet Lysander. He's my hornbill.'

He opened a door to the side of the kitchen, called out, 'Lysander!' and in came a big bird with a long curved beak and an orange head, walking like a little man. I sprang backwards into the table as it said, 'ARRRK!' My hands automatically crossed my chest. Lily laughed.

'ARK AK AK!'

'Visitors, Lysander,' Mr Clemm said. 'Behave, now.'

Lysander. A bit like a parrot, a bit like a toucan, but not quite like either. *That monstrous bird ... Spiteful-looking creature*, Mr Lombard had said. This was *that* bird. I wanted to laugh. I wanted to laugh so much, it hurt. I put a hand over my mouth and glanced at Lily, who was doing the same.

'Do you take him for night walks sometimes?' I asked. 'Because I was looking through my window once and thought I saw you with a bird ...'

'Oh, no – that wouldn't be Lysander. That's Godrell. He's a great bustard. He likes to go for midnight walks. Doesn't get on with Lysander, though, so he lives outside. Only comes in for the odd treat.'

Lysander shifted slowly from one foot to the other as Lily held out her hand and made clicking noises. He swivelled his eyes between all of us without moving his head, then looked straight at me and bit my jeans gently with the tip of his beak. He tugged. I kept still and smelt his warm, vinegary scent. Then he let go and locked eyes with Lily, but his beak stayed open.

'He just likes to get acquainted,' Mr Clemm said.

I couldn't wait to see who would look away first – nobody can outstare Lily – but Lysander went to stand right next to her, almost underneath her, and Lily grinned at all of us.

'Oh,' said Mum, 'he's found his lady, hasn't he?'

'Perhaps you'd like to see the capybara? They're just out the back here.' Mr Clemm took Mum and Lily out the back way with their tea, leaving the door open, and leaving me in the sticky heat of the kitchen. Lysander followed. I saw what looked like super-heavyweight guinea pigs in a pen, and soon Mum and Lily were totally occupied.

And then Mr Clemm returned to me and my heart speeded up and I felt myself getting even hotter.

'So,' he said. 'About our project.'

I stood there in a daze. How was I doing this? I didn't know what to say. The tea smelt like perfume. I told myself to be brave, but my thoughts went all watery and useless. The kitchen smelt of coffee, old fruit and warm, summer-baked furniture. Julia stared at me as if she knew everything. She kept so still. Her tail twitched every few seconds, but that was it.

'She likes you,' Mr Clemm said. 'Don't you, Julia?' (Mum's right about the way he speaks: he runs his words right to the ends of his breath, *Don'tttt youuu, Juliaaa?*)

Gently, I smoothed the back of Julia's head until she purred loudly, deep in her throat. My hand vibrated. She felt warm, like a hot-water bottle. On the wall above Julia's head there was a framed photo of a monkey. Mr Clemm saw me staring at it.

'Yes, that's Ashna. She died two years ago, but she had a good life here first,' he said. Then, as if he'd read my mind, he added, 'Somebody rescued her from a circus in India, and I rescued her from his cage. She couldn't have survived in the wild by that stage.'

He rummaged in a cupboard, then offered me a biscuit. He was still spider-like when he moved, but more daddy-long-legs than crouching spider. The Cloaked Strider was giving me a biscuit. *So unreal.*

I took a ginger nut and saw my own hand shaking. And then he said in a soft voice, 'You know, I'm not trying to imprison her.'

He sat down. So did I. He smelt of tobacco and clean feathers, like he'd come straight from stroking a hundred birds. Better now he wasn't towering over me quite so much.

'We seem to be caught in the same conundrum, you and me,' he said. 'Our speedy friend is causing havoc.'

I said, 'I've been calling her Whizzy,' but the word came out as a croaky whisper.

'Whizzy!' He leaned back in his chair and laughed. 'A fine name. Yes! Very apt indeed.'

'How does she make it rain?' I blurted. I'd decided to hurl my words out before they could go wrong, but it only seemed to make my heart race faster. 'And thunder and … everything?'

'Well, I think she has to manipulate her environment just to move through it,' he said. 'Who knows what by-products are released? Heat creates thunderstorms, and the temperature at her core will be phenomenal, like lightning. She can't help most of it. Often, she's just overexcited.'

'Where did she come from?' I asked.

He looked at me without replying. I got the feeling I was doing a test. There were no questions in it, so not sure how I was going to pass or fail, but he was definitely working me out.

'Let me show you something of what I'm trying to do, Alfie – come through to the workroom.'

Mr Clemm glided out of the kitchen – a floating walk, as if bits of him might come loose – and I followed him through a hallway where his coats hung, huge and long, like people waiting in the gloom.

The next room was full of tools and machinery. Papers and magazines spilt everywhere. Nothing looked new. Nothing was neat. By the door, it smelt like the inside of Mum's medicine drawer. Further in, the smell changed to oil and sawdust and old paint in metal tins. And Mr Clemm changed too. He seemed easier, more relaxed in here.

Mr Clemm sat down and rested his elbows on the bench, rubbed his chin, and gave me a long considering look. Then he said, 'She came down in a storm two years ago.' Even folded up, his arms looked gigantic. 'And it took me a long time to understand what happened in that storm. She came down in a big flare-up from the sun – a *coronal mass ejection*, they call them. There was a power cut all over the country, and the *aurora borealis* – the northern lights – could be seen in Folding Ford, which is almost unheard of. Curtains of light. Beautiful colours.'

Mr Clemm looked *so* different now. His face was lit up and he was actually smiling. He could never look normal, but suddenly, I got it: he looked *happier*. Maybe he was glad to be talking about Whizzy. Perhaps he was tired of keeping her a secret.

From the kitchen, Lysander did a quick, short squawk, and I saw that Mum and Lily had followed him back inside. Apart from raising his eyebrows, Mr Clemm ignored it. I had no idea what a coronal mass ejection even was, but he explained it really well. So it's what happens when the sun's magnetism gets in a knot and snaps like an elastic band.

Lily thinks I didn't see her listening in, but I did. She's always clever about this. She gets an expression on her face that would make Mum think she was totally present and listening to her, but she wouldn't be; her attention would be somewhere else. Lily can listen to two conversations at once.

'That's what happens far away in the sun,' he said, 'but down here, it was as if the sky bent over and kissed the ground, just for a second. But in that second, something blew in.'

His voice was very soft now – not far from a whisper. And I was getting used to the way he pronounced everything. There was no way Lily was catching all of this. I felt a bit sorry for her.

Whizzy had blown into *his* garden on the solar wind, *from the sun*.

26

Tunnels from the Sun

The best thing about finding out everything you've ever wanted to know is that it makes your brain go into a dizzy, tingly kind of shock. A *nice* shock. Everything in Mr Clemm's workroom stood out in dazzling shapes and colours, as if my eyes had turned superhuman. And I completely forgot to be nervous, because this intel was just so staggering.

Freakily, it might even be Mr Clemm's fault Whizzy's here – he's not sure. The solar wind blew her into Earth's orbit, but one of his magnetic devices might have pulled her down to earth. (I didn't dare ask him what that device was supposed to be *for*.)

'She protected herself inside some kind of casing back then – a strange ballooning thing, like plaster of Paris that's only just set. I thought of it as a healing cocoon. Or perhaps it was a stage in her life cycle.' He said this so quietly, it was almost as though he was talking to himself. 'I rolled her on to a big plastic sheet and took her into one of the barns. I looked after her.'

My questions came tumbling out quite smoothly after that. How could anything live in the sun? How could eyes stand those temperatures, even if they're made of something strong?

He'd had to do a crash course in thermodynamics and electrical engineering. And maybe Whizzy didn't come from the *actual* sun itself – he doesn't know. Maybe she came from the magnetic *field* of the sun, because there are magnetic tunnels between Earth and the sun, and those won't be as hot. But he's only guessing.

He rummaged in a drawer, pulled out a paper and passed it to me. 'I caught her here on infrared.'

The image was really grainy and shimmered like pearls, but Whizzy's shape was there.

'Wow,' I said, and we both stared at her for seconds. Down the hall, the kitchen had gone very quiet.

'These frilly things down her sides – I think they're organs for detecting rotation, acceleration, pressure and gravity. I'd had a friend from Cuba staying with me just before all this happened, and he used to talk a lot about the way different animals and fish sense things. There are more ways of sensing the world than the ordinary ones that we know about, Alfie.'

'But she's got eyes. They're like mirrors.'

He let quite a few seconds go by before answering. 'Yes, but she's not alone there. A species of fish has mirrors instead of lenses in its eyes, you know.'

(I didn't know. Sam is going to freak right out when I tell him this. He's going to get back to normal with me, for definite.)

'Who knows how sensory organs survive such temperatures?' he said, shrugging. 'Maybe metals are involved – but that's just a guess.'

I told him how I'd felt her reading me, as though she was building a vibration picture of me, and Mr Clemm looked seriously fascinated. We talked for ages. We decided, together, that Whizzy's eyes might even be three or more sense organs in one, and she might see with the help of vibrations like snakes do, and everything in Ash House was so easy now that I couldn't believe I'd ever been worried. I didn't want this perfect day to end.

When I asked how he knew Whizzy was female, he laughed. 'Sorry, Alfie – I don't know that at all. It's just a guess. I couldn't carry on calling her an "it", so I settled on "she". There may or may not be such a thing as male or female where she comes from – but I feel she's female.'

There are *rivers* in the sky, Mr Clemm told me! I wanted to text that to Sam straight away, but couldn't, obviously – that would have been rude. (And now I've decided face to face will be best so I can watch his mind blow.) *And* there are tornadoes on the sun – Mr Clemm showed me pictures of them on my phone.

And *I* told *him* that on Saturn, it might rain diamonds, and I can't be sure, but I think that's what set Lily off. I said 'diamonds' pretty loudly because I was all excited, and she turned her head like she'd been slapped. Sometimes things that people say remind Lily of whatever it was that happened to her, and there's no avoiding it because only Mum and Dad and Lily know what happened. So you say something totally innocent and she just flips. In any case, the next time I looked at her and Mum sitting back in the kitchen again, Lily had pulled a section of hair loose and was chewing the ends, and Mum was shaking her head vigorously and stroking Lily's arm while Lysander swayed from one leg to the other on the kitchen floor, scattering papers with his wings – *flick, flick, flick* – like he was sorting them into piles.

Mr Clemm hadn't noticed. 'I thought about feeding her electricity,' he said, 'but at first, she did quite well on sunlight itself. Sunlight is energy. But after a few weeks, she weakened.'

My heart skittered.

'I experimented. I used magnetite – that's a mineral found in rocks – and she liked it. I made the housing for her as you know, and lined it with magnetite, and set up a solar-panelling arrangement to give her energy, but every time I let her out, the time she lasted before collapsing grew shorter and shorter. In the end, I daren't let her loose at all. I just left her to rest.'

I knew Lily was going to flip out and demand to go home any second, but there was so much to tell him, and even more to find out. I told him about Whizzy nursing Lily, and his eagle-owl eyebrows shot up in amazement.

'So, she's changing again.' He whistled and stared at the wall for a few seconds. 'Astonishing.'

Tickly shivers ran up my spine as I realised something: I've got much further with Whizzy than Mr Clemm has. The room was silent for a while, and then he laughed excitedly.

'I knew I was right not to intervene. I knew you'd be just what she needed. That's why she shows herself to you and you alone. Will you let me know as soon as she returns to your house?'

I nodded madly.

'I read everything I could. She needs to keep her body stable in such a *very* different environment. As you've seen, when she's restless, the weather gets wild and a little bit strange, even when she's safely contained in the housing I made for her. And now that she's so much stronger, that old box wouldn't do a thing. Which is why we need this new machine.' He patted a very long, shiny box with lots of grooves down the sides and buttons that would probably light up. 'Just waiting for a new part because it isn't powering up properly. I've found a garage in the city that specialises in electrical components for cars, and I'm going to adapt an alternator!' He grinned. 'When that comes, I'll be able to move her to somewhere more remote. Maybe the Scottish Highlands. This village isn't suitable for her. She's a danger to all of us.'

'I know.'

'But don't worry, Alfie – I'll keep you involved in all our plans. You'll still be able to see her.'

I stared at a green velvet chair under the window that was bloated with masses of padding, except for the seat. You could see the dip where Mr Clemm had been sitting on it for years. I needed to ask him something, but I wasn't sure I wanted to know the answer. I took a deep breath.

'How strong can she get? It's pretty scary at the moment. Will it get even worse? Because it's been awful. My best friend isn't speaking to me because Whizzy sent everyone's tempers bonkers and his grandad got hurt in a big, stupid mix-up.'

He thought about this for a long time before answering. Then he said, 'I think we should assume it will. But I'm working as quickly as I can. All you need to do is be careful.'

Now Lily was smoothing her hair back over and over, then rubbing her eyes. Mum took hold of her by the shoulders and she stopped it. 'Alfie,' Mum called. 'Time to go.'

It was way, way too soon.

Then I felt brave enough to ask my final important questions. First, what was going on with all the moths? How had Mr Clemm got them on the threads?

Mr Clemm laughed. 'Ah! Yes. We almost met, didn't we? I remember that day. I was trying to take some of them out of Whizzy's range so they could fly away. The moths produce the threads themselves when she's around. The stuff they extrude is more like gossamer than silkworm silk. They love the electricity but end up trailing strings everywhere.'

Then finally I asked him why Mr Lombard hates him so much, and it was almost too late because Mum was already walking towards us, and Lily was leaving by the back door.

Mr Clemm scraped the edge of the bench with his thumb-nail and sighed. 'I made mistakes. He was badly affected by some pests I inadvertently brought back from Borneo. I've apologised, but some people won't accept apologies.'

'What about the spinal cords? Those seemed to get on his nerves a lot.'

Mr Clemm laughed. 'Leavings from my birds of prey,' he said. 'There've been rather a lot of those.'

'A lot of birds of prey, or a lot of spinal cords?'

His next laugh was louder. 'Both.'

Mum was standing there with strained eyes and a *let's go* look around her mouth. Lysander had followed her through and said, '*HA... HA... HAA!*'

We walked home, catching up with Lily, who'd stomped on ahead, and Mum told me precisely nothing about why.

<u>*3.15 p.m.*</u>

It's not going to be easy to phone Sam, what with Lily's big ears around the place, but I'm going to the bottom of the garden to try, because this new intel is really going to mend things with me and him. I am floating in a bubble of awesomeness, and when I think about Whizzy wrapped in her soft, wet, light-grey cocoon, my heart melts.

And as for Mr Nathaniel Clemm – he's marvellous! I still think he's ultra, uber, *well* weird, but I really, really like him.

Sam didn't pick up.

I tried for a few minutes, then messaged the whole Ash House visit to him. It took me ages and ages.

And he still didn't reply.

That must be it then, I thought. No more Lilac Farm. No more trundling down the farmyard in go-carts, no more bombing over the BMX ramps. No more messing about on the hay bales, making a massive racket for Sam's mum.

'If you make loads of noise, she doesn't need to keep checking we're still alive,' Sam had told me the first time I went to his house.

'So we could mess with real swords or guns, but as long as we shout our heads off all the time, she'll think we were safe!' I'd said.

He rolled his eyes, but he liked my crazy. Or so I thought.

Can't believe how things are now.

_7.15 p.m._

Lily had another twenty questions for me over supper. Why was Mr Clemm telling me about massive elastic bands in the sky? Were we creating a sci-fi story together, and what about the animal I was supposed to be looking for?

Mum said, 'It sounded like an eel from what Mr Clemm was saying. But that's impossible – he's only got a pond, so he'd easily keep track of an eel.'

'I know that, but what's it got to do with the northern lights and electricity?' Lily said. 'And why does it need solar panels?'

I sighed. 'I might have found out the answers to all those questions if you'd let us stay a bit longer!'

'I know,' she said and, to my UTTER astonishment, lifted a gentle hand and ruffled up my hair. Then she sighed the deepest sigh I've ever heard. 'I just got upset and had to leave. Sorry.'

I was stunned. Mum looked like she was holding her breath while pretending to be normal.

'That's OK,' I said. Then we smiled funny little sad smiles at each other.

Really wanted to ask her about the diamonds, but just couldn't do it – it was totally the wrong moment. But I'll file that word away, and one day I'll have enough other stuff to put with it to make something sensible.

8.30 p.m.

Dad video-called just now. Mum went first because she had boring house stuff to tell him, but then she went straight into everything about Mr Clemm that I'd planned to say.

'Quite a character underneath the eccentricity,' she said. 'Mind you, he's not above smuggling the oddest animals into the country on boats with the help of other militant conservationists, when the need arises.' She said this in a low voice, like it was a dodgy secret.

Dad said something I couldn't hear, then Mum said,

'No, he gives intensive one-to-one care, then transfers them to good zoos.'

Thought maybe I could be a militant conservationist one day, but that was before I looked it up. It's nothing to do with the army.

My turn came last, but Mum had ruined it. The order I'd planned to say everything in just collapsed.

'Hey,' Dad said. 'Lily's full of cute geese and a bird that walks like a little man!'

'It's a hornbill.'

'With the brain of a ten-year-old human, Lily says.'

'She's exaggerating,' I said. 'But yeah. I was mostly busy talking.'

'To the big man?'

'Yep.'

'Proper zoo, he's got,' Dad said. 'Do you think it cheered Lily up?'

'Probably.'

So neither of the others have told Dad about the diamond thing. Good thing I held off, then. Sometimes it's hard to get it right.

And Dad hasn't even noticed that I've stopped sending him bits of my journal.

27

How to Ruin Your Life

<u>*14th August*</u>

I'm getting ready for Sports Camp on the recreation field. Don't want to go, but Mum says I have to, and I need to go early to help the coach set up.

'It'll go towards your bank of good turns,' she said. 'Of which you need plenty more—'

'*More?* How many sorriments do I have to make?'

'Sam should be there,' she said. 'You might get a chance to build bridges.'

That's if Sam even turns up.

<u>*5.30 p.m.*</u>

Something really stupid and frightening and accidental

just happened. Mum's stunned. She's upstairs now, and I think she might be having a lie-down. It started on the recreation field.

Sam did turn up for the Sports Camp. He didn't look at me all morning, and his whole body said *back off*. During the first penalty shoot-out, my stomach tightened and twisted. It was like trying to play football with open warfare going on in my guts. After lunch, we got pushed together in the pavilion, supposedly to bring out the equipment for the ball-control session.

We hadn't been in the same room together for two weeks, and the silence stretched between us like a sheet of something filthy.

Couldn't stand it for long. I had to speak. 'How's your grandad?'

For a few horrible seconds I thought he wasn't going to answer. But then he said, 'Same.'

I nodded. 'What did you think of all the intel I got from Mr Clemm?'

He shrugged, turned away and went outside carrying two cones, leaving me completely flattened. That was my best shot. I followed him outside with more cones, but every time I tried to get near him, he walked away. I had to stop. I looked like a stalker.

And then a piece of total intergalactic amazement

happened – my heart's still doing a quadrillion extra beats because of it. Whizzy joined us. Right in the middle of the tackling-skills session!

It started with an unbelievably loud buzzing that came from my phone, as if a text was landing, but much deeper, like a church organ would throb if it could get inside a phone. It attracted everyone's attention. Slipping off to our pile of bags and coats behind the touchline, I pulled it out of my bag and now it ticked, like a clock. *Ticka-tick thrum. Ticka-tick thrum*. It couldn't be. Whizzy? *In my phone?*

The coach waved his arms at me. 'Turn that off and put it away, please, Alfie.'

I pretended to do as I'd been told. Everyone stared. Sam glowered.

The ball-control drills continued, but so did the mega-buzzing, and I ended up leaving the pitch three times.

'Alfie, what on earth are you doing?' the coach said, coming over to me. 'Your phone should be off! Get rid of it immediately and focus!'

My cheeks burned. 'I need a break, Mr Mason.'

'Not now, Alfie – we've just got started!'

'Please, I feel a bit strange.'

One of the other boys sniggered.

'OK,' Mr Mason said. 'Take five, everyone.' He crouched

down so we were on the same level. 'You're Alfie *Bradley*, aren't you?'

I nodded.

'Look,' he said, 'you've got yourself a bit of a reputation as a disruptive element, so watch it, OK? This is a warning – if you're genuinely poorly, I'll phone your parents and send you home, but mess me about one more time, and you're out. Is that clear? You don't look ill to me. You look full of beans.'

'I'll be fine in a minute,' I said, but my head was reeling. Was nowhere safe from Mr Lombard's tentacles?

'Have a drink of water, then get back to it.'

I nodded, pocketed my phone, and headed for a big patch of mown grass that was turning into hay. It was well away from everybody else. All the way there, my pocket fired out more pulsing, and when I took it out, the screen was white with grey dots all over it: a very ill-looking screen. Near the bottom, something like a hole shimmered and swirled. White whiskery tendrils leaked from it.

Seconds passed. The tendrils folded up to nothing, then reappeared and whooshed to the edge of the screen, where things carried on out of sight. Fast things. I could *just* see the edge of what was going on.

Then Whizzy came gushing into clear view – long and stringy and bright, like a wild, frantic pink candle flame with a seahorse's head. Major unreality. Felt like I might burst. The feeling got stronger and stronger as Whizzy got clearer and brighter and more brilliantly wonderful than I can describe.

'Hello,' I said gently. 'How have you got inside there?'

Whizzy corkscrewed slowly around the arrow on the *Slide to Unlock* bit, and a tiny noise vibrated through the phone. I brought it closer to my ear, and it was awesome – musical – but Whizzy was whirling too fast, so sound and picture were both blurred. She was just playing. Playing in my phone.

This felt fantastic. Now Sam could see her properly and – I caught my breath – this was going to solve *everything*.

I ran over to Sam.

'You were right, Sam! You were dead right!' I said. 'The compression and unzipping along wires, and all that other science stuff you said – she's done it! Whizzy's in my phone! Come on!' And I ran back over to my patch of grass, hoping he'd follow. Surely he had to forgive me now?

He did follow. He was slow, and looked confused and annoyed, but he came.

I shoved the phone right up to his face, so close that he flinched. 'Look at *this!*' I said, and I edged round so I could see too. The entire screen was rippling. Brilliant white ridges ran across the top half, then fizzed down to nothing but a tiny *S* shape against a grey background: Whizzy. She was small, in the bottom-right corner under the mail icon, but growing.

Sam's eyes were the brightest I've ever seen them. 'What happens when you tap her?' he whispered.

I did, gently, and a blizzard of white dots poured out over my finger. She disappeared. I swiped across and there she was, swirling all over the place leaving trails of pink light, electric-looking, like a plasma lamp I once had.

Whizzy grew and grew. The icons were mostly blotted out.

Sam didn't move. He just stared. 'Wow, Alfie,' he breathed. 'Incredible. Like a dream.'

I nodded. 'But we're awake!'

His mouth was stiff with surprise and stayed open a bit, as if he was expecting a spoonful of food.

'Do you think she travels like a text?' I asked him, still speaking just above a whisper. 'And where do you think she actually is? In the screen, or bombing about in the circuit board?'

He shrugged and raised his eyebrows, as if surprised I'd even heard of such things.

'Dad told me how a smartphone works,' I said, staring down at Whizzy. 'How do you squash up so small?' I whispered to her. 'And you're quiet now. Must be getting used to it.'

'Such eyes,' he said. 'They *are* like mirrors. And you were right – she is like a sunhorse. A total sunhorse.'

'I'll have to tell Mr Clemm she's in here,' I said. Sam looked at me. 'But not just yet.'

'Should I text you? To see what happens?'

I nodded and he raced to get his phone. When the text arrived, she shrank again, dived on to it and rode away as it scrolled off-screen.

'I've lost her!' I said.

'Here, let me see.' Sam took the phone and scrolled around. 'Look! She's in your Contacts.'

Whizzy was weaving in and out of all the letters in Dad's name. Then I opened Sam's text properly, and instead of words, there was an image. It looked like an inside-out snow-flake from a kaleidoscope – everything was backwards.

'Unreal!' Sam said. 'Now you text me!'

I scrolled back to Sam's contact. Whizzy followed me. I typed *awesome*, and as it started to send, there was a burst of white light, like she'd loaded the phone with stars.

Mr Mason's voice boomed across from the football pitch. 'Sam Irwin! Alfie Bradley! Come on – we're all waiting.'

Sam's cheeks turned red as fast as if someone had swiped them with a paintbrush. 'Right, better put her away for now. Leave your bag here, yah?' he said bossily, but his eyes said something else.

The battle was won. He loved Whizzy now.

In the end, we left the phone in the hay, well covered up, and took my bag back to the touchline. It was murder having to go through a whole football tournament when all we wanted to do was see Whizzy, but it felt so good to be back with Sam. And if we could keep Whizzy safely in the phone, I could start to relax and enjoy myself. Maybe my phone had even saved the village!

When camp finished, we dived back to our mini hayfield and concentrated on Whizzy. The recreation field was filling up with kids and parents.

'Look,' he said, as we crouched down together, 'she's horizontal.'

'She's done that nearly every time I've met her. I thought there must be something in the ground she needed, but that can't be right if she's doing it in the phone.'

'Maybe she's finding electricity in there,' Sam said, 'or something magnetic. There's gold in phones, and rare elements and stuff. Maybe she can use those if she gets flat enough.'

'Or maybe she's got gas,' I said, grinning. 'As soon as I get horizontal, I want to fart.'

We spent about a minute laughing at that before Sam

realised gases probably do come with Whizzy somehow and got deadly serious again.

'I know,' he said, his voice getting louder and squeakier. 'Try leading her on to my contact and then call me – see if she comes across into my phone with the call! Then I could take her home with me.'

'But … maybe you could just come to my house for the night instead.'

'No,' he said, lining his phone up against mine. 'I want to see if this works. *I* want to be alone with her, for once.'

'OK,' I said, but I had an uneasy feeling. Did I want Sam to take Whizzy home? No. Not really.

We both looked at her. She was coiled around the date at the top right of the screen, moving slowly, lazily, eyes looking out at us.

'She looks sleepy,' I said.

Sam put his finger over her gently, and tried to drag and drop her on to the Contacts icon. But Whizzy just brightened into a blinding white, then turned deep indigo. Beautiful, but moody. He couldn't drag her, not even a millimetre. Suddenly, I realised something.

'That's the colour she goes when she's cross, or getting ready for a fight,' I said. 'Normally she's white-gold. She's pink when she's playing … but *that* colour –' I shook my head – 'she's not gonna be tame any time soon. Not if she's that colour.'

Sam chewed his lips. 'You try,' he said.

I did, and Whizzy shot to the opposite corner of the phone each time my finger landed on her. It was as if she knew.

Sam didn't look at me.

We tried everything. We sent text after text to each other, but she scattered into pieces with each text now, and there was a popping, whistling sound before she went back to normal. I felt my face getting hotter and hotter.

'Just scroll to my contact and call me anyway, even if she won't come to start with,' Sam said. 'Once we've got her used to the sensation, we might be able to pass her backwards and forwards between us.'

I did. The *Sam* icon tilted and wobbled, and when he answered his phone, his voice boomed down from the sky so loud, it was like being clobbered around the ears.

(((HELLO)))

We gaped at each other, and then he punched *End Call* quickly, but kids came running across from the zip wire under the trees. My eardrums throbbed. It felt like they might snap.

Sam frowned at me. Something else was wrong. A heavy

pressure had settled on the field. It pushed against the top of my head. The curious kids had stopped a few metres away from us and now just stared.

Sam stood up. He glanced across at the distant adult heads bobbing by the bowling green. 'Come on, Alfie – we'll just go to mine now.'

My phone was hot and getting hotter. I panicked and turned it off.

Bad idea. A blue flash zigzagged from the phone to the sky. *Right up*. It took a fraction of a second – too fast for most eyes – and it was completely silent. Not even a *whoosh*. My ears popped, but that was it.

She was out. And now the phone looked like a firework in my hand. Tubes of light twirled out of it like white-hot spaghetti.

'Alfie, what …?'

My hand was burning, so I dropped it. Within a micro-second, the spaghetti-tube light caught hold of the hay and absolutely fried it. The whole place was so dry, it burst alight.

'Unbelievable!' Sam yelped, stamping on the hay. 'Something happens every single time!'

The fire started to weave little paths through all the dry stuff, first in one direction, then another. I stamped, but it flared up around my feet.

The little crowd of kids moved closer. Someone said, 'Put it out!'

'I'm totally trying!'

Sam hissed, 'Oh no, no, no!' And I carried on stamping. The fire took no notice. I danced about.

Sam emptied out a bottle of lemonade, but only killed about a centimetre. The rest of the fire flared up worse than ever. His forehead was as sweaty as mine and his lips were a thin, scared line.

I looked up, and there was Whizzy, hovering but small again, which was just as well – but everyone was looking at the fire. She was all jazzed and jerky. You could tell she was sorry. Then she shot to the top of one of the football flood-lights and fed herself right inside it.

I felt sick. 'Didn't mean this to happen.'

And then someone from the bowling green came towards us carrying a fire extinguisher. Stiff brush-like side hair. Footsteps that scraped the ground, even here.

My face got even hotter. 'Oh no, it's Lombard! This is going to be Strike Three.'

Sam said nothing. He looked like he was about to puke.

'Maybe if you tell him it wasn't my fault. He likes you.'

Sam stuck his hands in his pockets and hunched his shoulders. He cleared his throat, and in a small, tight voice said, 'Sorry, Alfie.'

'Sam! Back me up!'

But he walked away.

I was left with a furious Mr Lombard, who put out the fire in a blast of white powdery smoke from the extinguisher.

'You again!' he said to me when it was done. 'So gnashing about on private property got boring, did it? Moved on to public spaces, have you? Going in for *extreme* vandalism this time?'

'No, I didn't start this fire – it was an accident! My phone overheated and—'

'I know your type,' he said. 'Knew it as soon as I clapped eyes on you.'

My phone had fizzled out by now. Shaking my head at Mr Lombard, I pocketed it. Despite the foam from the extinguisher, it was dry. Dread filled my lungs like a horrible sticky weight.

I forced my shaky legs to move and started to walk away, but Mr Lombard took hold of my arm. 'You're going nowhere, my lad.' His spit rained down on me.

'It's fine now,' I said, shrugging him off. My voice was thin and broken.

'What you call "fine" could have spread to the pavilion, the bowling-green hut, the trees – the whole field could have gone up. What you call "fine" could have ended up costing a lot of parish council funds, not to mention the time and money of the fire services. What if you'd set yourself on fire? This really is the final straw.'

I said nothing and backed away. Couldn't tell them what really started the fire, could I? They wouldn't believe me for a second, and if they did, it would be even worse for Whizzy. What might they do to her? I couldn't betray her.

At first, I thought Mr Lombard was going to let me go, but he followed, pointing a finger at me. 'You're going to the devil, son.'

'It wasn't even my fault!' I yelled at him. I couldn't help it. Angry tears were prickling, and my face was running with sweat. 'It was a total accident with my phone! Ask Sam Irwin – he was with me!'

'Bringing innocent people into your lies won't help you.'

I shook my head – it was all so hopeless. But Whizzy must have felt my torture because dark purple flashes snaked through the grass around my feet. They were minute, no bigger than a hair. I glanced back at Mr Lombard and he was still coming slowly, still chuntering and still probing me with his baking hot stare every step of the way. '*No, Whizzy,*' I hissed from the corner of my mouth. '*Ignore.*'

I broke into a run and headed for home, but Whizzy didn't give up. I'd only got as far as the river bridge when a noise came from somewhere close to the ground. It was a long, deep, angry musical note. And then Whizzy's anger shot straight up to the sky again, scattering birds.

For a split second she seemed to be as big as the world – as if the whole sky had taken a huge white-gold breath – and my heartbeat got so heavy and fast, it filled my throat. In that second, she seemed to be pulling at something I couldn't see. *Yanking*, with a horrible strength. Whizzy was heaps stronger now. She was terrifying. And then she vanished.

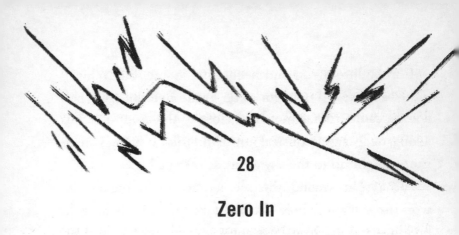

28

Zero In

<u>*6.30 p.m.*</u>

The knock at the door came in the middle of tea. Mum was annoyed before she even answered it. She'd only just sat down and lifted her first forkful – it hadn't even reached her mouth.

Two police officers – a man and a woman.

'It's very serious, young man,' said PC Banik, the woman, when they were inside. 'And you're one of the boys involved in the allotment vandalism too, aren't you?'

How did they know about *that*?

I thought about Sam and what he'd done to me. I could say his name now, and tell them he'd been with me when the fire started. They'd go round to his house and question him too. I twisted my back and shoulders in my hot T-shirt and imagined Sam's face … and then said nothing.

'And some trespassing in a local smallholding?' PC Banik tapped the side of her head. 'Don't give us any reason to be knocking on your door again.'

_7.45 p.m._

I've been sitting in the garden for ages. The laptop isn't too glary now the sun's gone in, and it's cooler out here under the tree. My fingers are still shaking on the keyboard, but the rest of my body's stopped.

They're not going to take it any further because the fire service wasn't needed, but I have to sign something called a 'police caution'. And they looked at me strangely when they examined my phone.

'Nothing to suggest any unusually reflective surfaces,' PC Banik had said, and Mum had shaken her head as if she couldn't believe she wasn't dreaming. 'It needs to be returned to the manufacturer if it's getting hot enough to start fires.'

I told them it wasn't the actual phone, but they went on about magnifying-glass fires, and how it's best to be honest.

They've told Mum to keep a closer eye on me. That was one of the worst parts. She went red and I wanted to slither down a hole.

I remembered the park near my old house in the city, the patches of bare mud that had always made me feel fed up. The older boys there sometimes started little fires, tiny ones, in cans, or medium-sized ones for barbecues. My friend Chapal has a brother who could light them out of anything, out of nowhere.

I feel numb, like somebody's dipped me in a tank of ice. How could Sam do this to me?

Whizzy's totally gone and my phone's dead. Nothing happens when I charge it. Tried to phone Mr Clemm on the landline to tell him she *was* in my phone but now she's escaped, but there was no answer.

Can't stop thinking about how terrifying Whizzy had looked when she went humongous in the sky. And the *power* of her now. It's frightening. I felt it surging through my legs when she left the phone, and even now I still feel a bit zingy below the knees.

She really can't stay here, not like this.

And someone's written the word *BLOOD* on the back window of our car in the dust.

8.30 p.m.

Dad's just phoned. There was radioactive fallout. I was sitting with Lily on the sofa when Mum brought the phone in, and I thought he'd want to talk to Lily, but this time he wanted to talk to me first.

'I thought we were clear. I thought that box you found was in some kind of communal waste ground. But you've been going into private property?'

'Didn't mean to,' I said. 'And now the owner is fine with me, and he's given me a job to do.' Good thing I've stopped sending Dad those journal chunks.

'Is that so?'

'Yes.'

'What's the job?'

'To keep an eye out for a wild … thing that's escaped.'

'Mum said nothing about a job,' he said.

'No, well—'

'You had no right to worry Mum. We don't want a repeat of the key-posting business.'

Mum once posted the car keys (which have the house keys attached) into a letter box and kept the letter she was posting in her hand. That was when Lily was in hospital.

'*I'm* stepping in now. You are to stay at home where Mum and Lily can keep an eye on you. I thought I could trust you not to do stupid things. And dragging Sam into it with you is unforgivable.'

'I didn't drag him, and he wasn't even there at the

end – he legged it!' Just saying it made my throat feel like it was closing up.

Then Dad repeated everything he'd just said but in a louder voice. I held the phone away from my ear and kept saying *yes* and *sorry* and *I know* till he stopped, but it wasn't good.

And then he asked me to pass him to Lily.

Lily put the phone to her ear and her eyebrows shot sky high as she listened to Dad. And then she started totally blistering Dad's ear off in a way I never dreamed she'd dare.

'Are you still obsessing about me and my stuff?' she said to him. 'Because there's all this stuff going on with Alfie and you never give him any attention.'

'He just did,' I said. 'Too much.'

'Too late,' Lily said down the phone. 'Alfie has been completely neglected by you, and now – when he needs you most – you're not even *listening* to him! The fire was an *accident*!' Her voice was getting louder and louder. 'Can you *hear* me? Something is happening to *Alfie*, not to me. So get your act together and help him out, for once in your life!'

Couldn't hear what Dad replied because she didn't have him on speaker, but her last words were snapped out with pure venom:

'Fine, then! Do that!'

And then she hung up! On *Dad*!

She gave me a nod and walked away.

I couldn't even move for a few seconds – it felt like my whole brain had crashed. Lily was on my side! Totally and completely and awesomely!

Mum came in while I was still standing in a daze, and she looked pretty stunned too.

'Lily's just told me she's going to meet a friend from school,' she said, blinking again and again. 'She hasn't done that for the best part of two years!'

I opened my mouth, but no words came out.

<u>15th August</u>

Woke up feeling sick and awful from a nightmare – Whizzy died right in front of me. Her ripples turned into struggling movements in the dream, as if she was swimming in air as thick as honey.

Her eyes never left mine, but the light of her body dulled to silver, then to grey. She sank to the ground, quiet and still. Her eyes were like circles of grey glass in the end, and every nerve in my body was sobbing.

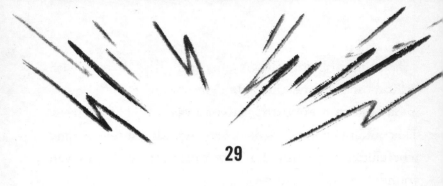

29

Beep

It all happened at five thirty this morning. I was dreaming about Sam's grandad – a half-awake, half-asleep nightmare – when a light flashed and woke me properly. All confused, I thought Sam and his grandad were in my bedroom, then the dream faded and something glowed on the ceiling – just for a second. I sat up and looked at the alarm clock, but it said 99:99 again.

Then the beam of white light was back, like a laser, and it came from my dead phone. Still tangled in the duvet, I picked it up and there was the home screen, all normal and working again, but with Whizzy diving through the internet icon like a rocket, twisting, fast and frenzied.

'W*aaay*, you've fixed it!'

Looking straight out at me from the screen with brilliant silver eyes, she pulsed importantly and showed me a kind of firework display in a picture of some trees. The phone beeped, then the whole screen turned into thick, dark churning smoke and I couldn't even see her.

I shrugged, still groggy. 'I don't get it, Whizzy. Is that a fire?' My stomach twisted into a knot. A fire she'd started?

The smoke picture faded. The internet closed down. Whizzy hovered for a few seconds, then zipped out of the phone and whizzed around my room manically.

'What's wrong? Don't wake anyone else, will you.'

She seemed gentle again, but it was hard not to think of how she'd been at the rec. That new power could really twist things up, rip stuff apart. I started shivering.

She fizzed faintly, like fizzy sweets popping on your tongue, but the sound seemed to come from inside my ears. The underneath of Whizzy was all fringed today, like a jellyfish, and a blue colour was slowly taking over from the fringing upwards. Really wild and wired now, she made frantic patterns in the air, leaving bristling silver trails, like sparkler writing. Did the shapes mean anything? Could they be diagrams? I tried to move my eyes fast enough to follow, but it was no good.

She zigzagged around the room again and made a

clicking noise, just like Dad's glasses when he folds them away – exactly that soft *click*.

'What do you mean?'

As if answering me, Whizzy changed from blue to star-white to milky white, and that sounds like a silly little thing, but it was amazing to see. And I had the feeling that she was trying to communicate with colours because the sounds hadn't worked.

'Wow, Whizzy. I don't get it, but wow.'

Her firework smell filled the room. She shimmied towards me and fluttered her semi-circular side thingies to a panicky blur. The dust particles in the air between us lit up and shivered like tiny sparks, and I flinched automatically because, really, she was still an actual runaway horse – wonderful but deadly.

She went to the top of my wardrobe and made herself small, then shot out of there, expanded herself to the height of my bedroom and turned round slowly. She did that over and over, like something was crucial.

'What's wrong? Has something happened?'

I was still whispering – I'm sure I was – but the next thing I knew, Lily was standing in my bedroom doorway with the hugest of all the almighty shocks in the universe sitting on her face, and Whizzy left through the window, too late. She travelled right through the glass itself, which made a scary sucking sound. And I don't know how I know this, but I'm sure she regretted going out that way.

At first we just stared at each other. Lily was pale – even paler than Mum – and when she spoke, her voice was tiny and wobbly.

'What was that?'

'Erm …' I said, then went quiet. My brain was whirring, but my body felt numb. 'You know that eel we've been talking about?'

She didn't take her eyes away from mine. 'That was not an eel.'

She stood in my room with her hands stuck to her cheeks, listening to me but looking like she might throw up. It took ages to tell her, because every few seconds she said, 'I'm getting Mum.' And I'd have to say, 'No, please don't, Lily!'

Then I'd explain again and try to persuade her why telling Mum *right at this moment* was a terrible idea, and how I absolutely must leave the house and follow Whizzy *immediately*.

'Just hold off, please,' I said. 'Trust Mr Clemm for a few more days.'

'Why don't *you* trust Mum? And Dad?'

'I do, but this is different.'

'No it isn't – it's serious. Does Sam know?'

And when she found out about Sam, she marched towards Mum's bedroom and I had to get hold of her arm and pull her away, all in frantic hissed whispers.

'Listen!' I said when I got her back in my room. 'You don't tell me everything, do you? What about the bullies? And the diamonds?'

'*What?*'

'You thought Mum had told me, didn't you? I guessed after what happened that day at Mr Clemm's. It's something to do with diamonds. *You* want to keep those kinds of secrets. Don't you?'

She shook her head, over and over, and stared at the floor. 'That's too horrible. And it's private. I might tell you one day, but ...'

'So you can see why sometimes people shouldn't be told things.'

She shook her head again. 'You're wrong about this. It isn't the same.'

And so I told her all over again about how Whizzy has been all summer, how Mr Clemm found her, and how he just wants to protect her from people who might harm her whilst also keeping the village safe from her wild fiery stuff, and how I seem to be the only person who can get close to her.

She looked up at me then, from my bed where she'd been sitting while I paced up and down. She was still pale, but seemed to be listening. And then I told her about Whizzy in the night, floating over her bed, and my nursing theory. Lily went very quiet.

'And now I'm going to Ash House to see what's wrong,' I said. 'Tell Mum I've gone to Mr Clemm's when she wakes up. Please only tell her that, for now. Please.'

Lily didn't look at me.

'Please. Lily.'

She didn't speak at first, but then she said, 'I thought it was a dream. For ages I've dreamed about something warm and bright that winds round and round everywhere for miles and miles and makes everything sparkly.'

She blinked. I breathed out and we stared at each other, both completely still.

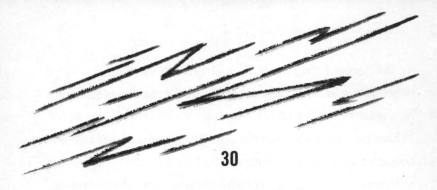

30

House of Ash

I'd spent the time it took to run out of Usher's Place phoning Mr Clemm. When there was no answer, I left a voicemail about Whizzy's behaviour, spilling out everything that had happened with Lily, my voice getting higher and faster and wilder: 'Whizzy didn't mean to be seen, but …' Lily won't tell, honestly …'

He didn't phone back.

Almost six-fifteen in the morning by now. Things felt wrong. The air was warm and windy, but the breeze sounded low to the ground, as if hunting something. Where was Whizzy? Hadn't she waited for me? At Malusky's Corner I looked behind me. Usher's Place seemed far away. The sky was huge and I felt tiny.

And then I saw her near the bottom of Raven's Rise, spiralling along close to the ground. I started running.

'Whizzy!'

She whizzed on ahead of me and I had to run flat out.

'Please wait! Whizzy!'

She did. She stopped outside the big house next to the bus stop and stretched herself up to about fifty feet tall. She was as thin as a piece of spaghetti and her insides glowed deep orange, and I lost my breath for a second – the sight was mind-blowing. Then she streamed off again towards Halfway Lane. I lost her, but surely she was going to Ash House.

I was at the turn-off to Halfway Lane when the first lights arrived in the sky. To begin with, I thought they were twisted shafts of very bright sunlight, but then the lights came together into one thick stem – and yes. It was Whizzy. And she was huge. Bigger than I'd ever seen her, and spinning herself around something. Something dark.

It took me a while to realise she was moving away from me. Away from Ash House. I kept my eyes on her until she was a tiny bright dot in the distance.

The white walls of Ash House glowed greyish in the strange early light, and the windows looked like black holes. I shivered.

The Bentley was still in the drive. The trees on the edge bent towards the house in the wind, and wisps of smoke curled around the side wall. I ran towards them, heart thumping wildly.

'Mr Clemm?'

I shouted it again and rounded the corner to more smoke, coming from the cellar, through the grate at ground level. Thick, grey, loads of it, puffing out like someone was blowing it from the inside. Like the picture Whizzy had shown me on my phone.

I screamed Mr Clemm's name again and hammered on the back door, then the front door. In the silence that answered me, and even over the sound of the wind, I could hear crackling. I called the emergency services, then ran away.

I ran till I couldn't feel my feet. The wind was against me, blowing back towards Ash House, so I had to fight to run. Wind clogged my ears, but it didn't stop me from hearing the explosion behind. I turned. Ash House was flaming along the wall closest to the trees.

Massive sobs broke out of me then – the kind where you gulp and gulp and every breath makes another sob. I had to stop running and bend over.

The noise of the sirens that came next – so fast – seemed to press against me just as much as the wind, and I hated it, even though I needed them to come and put out the fire. Two fire engines screamed towards me – and passed. I turned to run after them for about five steps before realising, and stopping: I had to get home.

Mum stood in the kitchen struggling to understand. 'And you told them Mr Clemm might be at home? When you phoned?'

I sat on a kitchen stool and nodded.

'Let's hope he wasn't in.' Mum looked confused. 'Nothing more you could have done in any case, darling. A miracle you were there to report it instantly.' She yawned. It was still so early. 'Why *were* you there?'

I looked at Lily and she shook her head quickly.

'I went to help him with his new machine.'

'Those machines! Probably what set the place alight. Oh, Alfie, imagine what could have happened to you! Amazing that you had the presence of mind to phone straight away without panicking – but just imagine! Doesn't bear thinking about.'

Lily went to the window and stood looking out for a long time. I found out that after I left for Ash House at stupid o'clock, she'd fallen asleep in my bed. Mum found her there, curled into a ball.

'Can you still see smoke, love?' Mum asked.

'Yeah,' Lily said. 'Not as much, though.'

They sounded far away.

After a while, Lily left the window and came to sit on the stool next to mine, looking like she wanted to do something, but didn't know what.

'I'm sure he'll have got out,' she said. 'Why wouldn't he? It's such a big house.'

'But what about Lysander? Julia's often outside. Godrell the great bustard lives outside all the time – so do the goats and capybara, so they'll be OK. But Lysander lives mostly inside …'

Lily didn't say anything. She just stared back at me with wide eyes, and my heart started beating faster and faster, each thud throbbing on an awful sick feeling that had been lying in my stomach since I got home. My next words were just squeaks: 'What if he's trapped?'

Lily started fiddling with her hair. 'We don't know that,' she said. Her voice was really definite, but her eyes stayed worried. She swallowed quickly, twice, and took a deep breath. 'There must be a door or window left open for him all the time, surely? He'd have to get outside to … to go to the toilet.'

'What if the new machine caught fire? Mr Clemm got a new part for it last week. What if it wasn't safe?' Tears burned behind my eyes.

She squeezed my shoulder. 'Someone will know soon. Stop imagining awful stuff.' She looked around. 'Where's …?'

'She went. Saw her go.'

'Where?'

I shrugged. 'To the horizon. Away.' My head had been sagging lower and lower since I pictured Whizzy leaving, and now it was down on the kitchen counter, resting on my arms.

Five minutes later, Lily had fetched Mum, and Mum had summoned Dad on video call and left me talking to him on the sofa, wrapped in a blanket. Mum came over every so often to rub my shoulders, but otherwise she left us alone.

'You had to get away – you got yourself to safety,' Dad said. 'You did the right thing to phone the emergencies and come home. I'm proud of you. We both are. You were so brave.'

'And now you need to rest and get over it,' Mum said. 'You're in shock, Alfie.'

I went back to bed and Mum brought me cereal, tea and toast to eat there. She was right. Sleepiness soon got me and took over.

_2.20 p.m._

The rest of today is dragging slowly on. Mum sent Lily to the shop to see what she could find out from asking people there, and she's come back with this:

1. *One wall of Ash House is virtually destroyed by a heat so fierce that experts are coming up from London to examine it.*
2. *They think one of Mr Clemm's machines blew up in the heat. (Bet I can guess which one.)*
3. *The rest of the house has been smoke damaged, but it's still standing.*
4. *Nobody knows whether Mr Clemm was in the house or not.*
5. *No news of Lysander or Julia.*

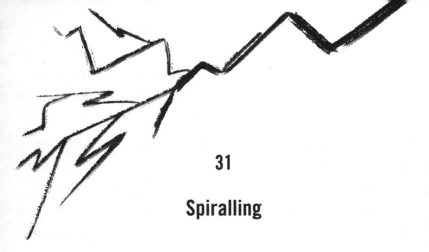

31

Spiralling

When Mum opened the curtains this morning, there was Julia, sitting on our garden wall and shaking something invisible off her front paw over and over again. Mum picked her up, brought her inside and gave her a tin of tuna.

That was the only good thing that happened today. As soon as Lily woke, she raced off to Ash House to look for Lysander and came back fifteen minutes later.

'The police are guarding everything,' she said. 'There are ribbons across the gate and around the house. Nobody's allowed in.'

I was in my pyjamas at the kitchen counter.

'The police have cordoned it off,' Mum said. 'That's huge.'

What happened next, while I was still in my pyjamas, is almost too unspeakable to write.

When those fire engines screamed towards Ash House, I thought it was the end of things, but I was wrong. It was just the beginning. The next part came when the police knocked on our door again. The same police.

They stayed longer this time. They told us the Ash House fire is suspicious and looks deliberate.

Mum pulled her hair out of its ponytail. 'That's terrible news, but what's it got to do with Alfie?'

'I'm afraid Alfie was the last person seen near Ash House, Mrs Bradley,' PC Banik said, and she frowned as Lily poked her head round the sitting room door.

Mum did a nervous little laugh. 'Alfie? But he found the fire. He called the emergency services …'

'What were you doing at Ash House so early this morning, Alfie?' PC Hislop started writing things down in a thick notepad. Lily slid into the room properly and stared at them from under her hair. It was her stare of obliteration.

'I went to see Mr Clemm, but he wasn't there. I saw smoke and phoned the emergencies … Then I came home.'

Lily nodded energetically. My stomach churned. I needed the toilet.

'He was first on the scene.' Mum's voice was high and scratchy. 'Without him, the place could have burned to the ground before anyone was alerted.'

PC Hislop stepped closer to me, stooped a bit, spoke gently. 'What did you do there, Alfie?'

'Nothing,' I said. 'It must have been Mr Clemm's new machine. It must have got too hot – or perhaps when he fixed it, something went wrong.'

Julia sat on the windowsill, watching everything with half-closed eyes.

'I'm afraid we suspect that the fire was started intentionally. So you can see that the situation is very serious indeed, Alfie.' PC Banik turned to Mum. 'Mrs Bradley, Alfie has already been cautioned for starting a fire on the recreation field just the other day. Mr Lombard, the head of the parish council, was on hand to deal with that fire and has reported his concerns about Alfie – concerns he's had for a good few weeks now. Alfie's been seen hanging around Ash House and its grounds on many occasions, and up to present, he's the last person to have visited the house before the fire started yesterday.'

I sank on to a chair, too floppy to stand. *There were two of us*, I could have said. I thought of the look on Sam's face when the flames started crackling. The panic in his eyes. I couldn't say it.

Mum looked like she was going to cry. Then she sprang into action. 'I've got to speak to our solicitor. *Now*. Nobody do anything until I've got her on the phone.'

'What about Dad?' I asked.

'One step at a time, Alfie.'

I could see myself reflected in the coppery metal frame of the fireplace. I looked scared. I looked like somebody else. I imagined myself bombing out of there, up the chimney like Whizzy, travelling high into the sky and folding around a cloud. I'd never come down again.

They stayed for about half an hour, asking me the same questions over and over, asking Mum things about where I went every day, and why, and who with.

After they'd gone, Mum gripped me by both shoulders and sank down to my level on the floor. 'Alfie, I want you to take deep breaths and stay calm. They have no right to come here with such ridiculous and dangerous accusations, when *you're* the one who discovered the fire and raised the alarm. We're going to sort this out, but you just have to believe that it's all going to be fine. There's been a stupid mistake.' She trembled. Her face was the palest I've ever seen it, and her eyes were furious.

Horrible, awful waves of terror covered me completely, and I started to sob.

And then Lily was on me and at me, fussing and flapping and jabbering endless words that blended into all the other sounds I could hear – the washing machine whirring and Mum on the phone and my heart still hammering in my ears. It took a while for me to come out of my shock and actually listen to her.

'I was accused of something I didn't do too,' she was saying. 'It was at a sleepover. Someone's mum's diamond earrings went missing … and – and … the day before it happened, I'd been trying them on. My friends believed the bullies.'

Her words went round and round my head. Some slid out.

'*Suddenly*, just like that, they … totally believed *them* – not *me* at all. After all those horrible months of nastiness, after everything the bullies did to me. And then I found one of the earrings outside where it'd been dropped – they were probably lost, not stolen.' She stopped to take a long, shuddery breath. 'It was just next to the family car. It was raining and everything was soaking, and … the diamonds in it were … They shone so brightly through the rain! They still glitter in my nightmares. You couldn't miss them – nobody could!' She began to gabble faster. I could hardly tell what she was saying. 'I left the earring there. Had to. Just went home. In all that rain. I knew if I picked it up and took it to her mum, they'd all think I was trying to return it, trying to pretend the other one was still lost. Because *I'd* found it, you see. Already, nobody believed me.'

So this was her awful secret. This was what they'd said about her, these were the words too bad to say aloud, even to Mum, for ages. Diamonds, tears, rain.

'Then it got on to social media and now I was this great big thief. *Not the first time*, they wrote. How clever is that? And s-someone made a cartoon of me –' she took another big breath – 'wearing the earrings … and so the bullies won.'

Lily yanked loose threads out of the cushion next to her, two at a time, fingers fast and savage. 'But Alfie, this can't … They can't do this to you …' She trailed off and sat still. 'I won't let them.'

I didn't speak, just stared at her, and she stared back at me.

We were double-stunned.

NEW JOURNAL

21st August, 11.15 p.m.

We thought there would be time between the police going and whatever was going to happen next.

But they came for me this afternoon.

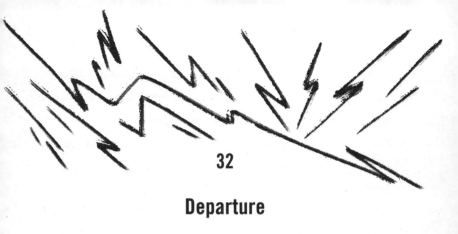

32

Departure

The houses on Usher's Place curve round in a semicircle, so when they came for me, there was no hiding. Faces appeared at windows, curtains jiggled, and things suddenly needed doing in front gardens.

The social worker – the most smiley lady ever – took me by the shoulders while two men stood beside the open car door, watching. She guided me forwards gently, but my stomach lurched, like it was trying to escape by itself. The rest of me was jelly.

Mum came too, but Lily had to stay behind. She stood on the doorstep with Mrs Gillespie, who's going to stay at our house for a while. When the social worker first put her hands on my shoulders, Lily looked ready to yank her fingers off me, one by one.

The social worker looked like she was used to this. 'Are

you comfortable?' she asked when we were all strapped in.

'Yes, thank you.' Mum's voice was thick and swamped with tears, as if she had a mouthful of porridge.

Then Lily took a step towards the car and shouted, 'You can't take him! Alfie!' And Mum had to get out of the car and calm her down, and then the social worker got out too and untangled Mum and Lily, and Mrs Gillespie put her arms right round Lily until she looked like a small girl.

Lily stopped shouting, but she didn't stop sobbing and sniffing.

By the time they got Mum back in the car, I couldn't listen to Lily any more. I covered my ears but kept my eyes on hers till the very last second.

33

Always Watching

Court was frightening and boring and confusing all at once. Adults spoke one at a time and took ages. Mum and I just sat there.

Then Mum had to go home and I had to carry on in the same car, away from her.

I'm never going to write about that.

They've taken my phone, so I can't get texts.

'Nothing bad is going to happen to you, Alfie,' the social worker said. 'We're just taking you to an appropriate setting until your case can be heard fully. That takes a little while to prepare. But there are other boys there and you'll soon settle in.'

Don't want to settle in. Just want to go home.

This place is called the Mandeville Centre, and it's the Appropriate Setting. There's a town somewhere close, but the Mandeville Centre is in the countryside. It's not a prison; it's a Secure Training Centre. Sounds like a college, doesn't it? It's not.

By the time I got here the sky was dark. I had to have my assessment straight away because it was so late, but they took ages to explain everything, because they were being so calm and slow. Nearly fell asleep, but halfway through explaining all the rules and routines, they brought me some toast and juice. And this new notebook.

They asked weird questions. What are my favourite hobbies, what scares or worries me. They aren't like teachers. They *notice* you, every inch of you, and they're always there. Always.

Then they took me straight to my room in the main building. I'm at the end of a long corridor on the ground floor, by myself. There isn't any upstairs here.

I'm wide awake now.

22nd August: 6.15 a.m.

I must have gone to sleep at least a little bit, because I

dreamed Ash House was nothing but ash. It fluttered in the breeze all over the village, like summer snow.

Woke up in a bed made of orange wood with a brown duvet in strange pyjamas. My eyes are scratchy and sore. The sun woke me. It seeped through the sides of the thin blue curtains. I knew it was early, because the building was silent, and this place is full of boys. Lots of them.

No idea who they are or what they look like, which makes me feel a bit sick. They're all asleep now, though. All except me.

Things I Wish I Hadn't Done:

1. _Listened to the scrap in the village hall. I should have gone home with Mum and Lily and a plateful of cupcakes instead._
2. _Gone near Tombard. Wish I'd never set eyes on him._
3. _Got caught up in Whizzy's hot-phone blaze on the recreation field. Of all the things I did, this was the worst. This was the one that really convinced them._
4. _Gone back to Ash House looking for Mr Clemm the day of the fire._

That's how many mistakes I made: four. And now Mr Clemm might be dead, the entire village thinks I'm a fire-starter, I can't talk to Mum or Dad or Lily, my best friend hates me, and I've ended up here. And where is Whizzy?

Going to explore now.

11.15 a.m.

The first corridor is really long, with fire-escape doors at each end. From the first door, you can see a brick wall, some small red brick buildings and a concrete yard.

The furthest fire door is better. From there, you can see a little garden with smallish trees and more buildings. I stared out for ages at the sky. I realised I was looking for a spark of light or a flash of pinky blue. But there was nothing.

Through another fire door and along another corridor, everything was still silent apart from a bluebottle flying in a square shape along the ceiling.

Nobody came, so I carried on to the main window in the entrance hall. Grey buildings stood on little stilts straight across from the main building. Loads of them, as far left and right as you could see. 'Appropriate Settings'. Not prisons.

I tried another door. Locked.

Then there were footsteps, soft ones, coming towards me.

'Good morning, Alfie – you're up and about early! How are you doing?'

It was a lady I hadn't met before, so not sure how she knew my name.

'Hello,' I said. My voice sounded high and thin.

'Breakfast isn't for a while yet, but we need you to be dressed before you eat it, so why don't you get ready quietly, then have a proper look around. It must feel horrible there with your cold, bare feet.'

It does feel horrible here, but my feet have nothing to do with it.

The dining room here is small compared to the one at school. Everyone piled in at the same time. I was the only new one, and the other boys stared. I sat next to someone with tramlines in his hair, who never spoke a word. One of them coughed all the time. It came out like a bark.

I had Weetabix and toast. Then the man who'd been watching over us at breakfast – Mr Francis – said, 'Jack, please can you lead out today,' and everyone followed this one boy out of the dining room, across the hall and through the front door into the open air.

I'd been dying to get out into the light, but in seconds, we arrived at one of the grey buildings on stilts. They'd looked like spare classrooms because that's what they were. We had school. I couldn't believe it. School in the summer holidays! It's barbaric.

The teacher, Mr Francis, is short with brown curly hair and a round face. There's something so smooth and peaceful about him. He reminds me of an actor from one of Mum and Dad's old comedy shows. He looks at us as if he expects fantastic things. Don't know how he's lasted in the job, because someone probably disappoints him every single day.

'OK, everybody – clean page,' he said. 'This is going to be a piece of persuasive writing. Title: "House of the Week". You are going to persuade people to buy this house. The trouble is, the house –' he paused and looked around with fake shock on his face – 'is Not Very Good. There are holes in the floor-boards. The plaster is crumbling from the walls. It's part of your job to think about what else might be wrong with this house and persuade buyers to purchase it anyway.'

I picked up my pen, but didn't write. I thought about Ash House.

Three walls charred, one wall rubble.

The roof blackened.

Ash blowing along Halfway Lane.

The sun came out and I stared through the window. Mr Francis came round and skimmed my blank paper.

'No thoughts yet, Alfie?'

34

Questions

24th August, 6.30 p.m.

They've brought a plate of sandwiches, a carton of fruit juice and some cream crackers to my room, because I wouldn't eat anything in the dining room. It's their fault. There were three of them and one of me. A social worker, Miss Hughes, who settled me in on my first night here, and another person I've never seen before who's come here especially for me.

Twenty million questions. It started straight after last lesson.

'Can you remember how you were feeling that day on the recreation field? Why you felt the need to light that fire?' The lady asking all the questions was small and thin with short dark hair and a smart black suit, like she'd come from an office.

The police asked me that fifty thousand times before I came here. 'It was an accident. I didn't *light* it. It says what happened in my journal. On my laptop. They took my laptop, so you must know—'

'Were you trying to impress somebody? Or were you just bored?'

'No.'

'You know how dangerous fire can be though, don't you, Alfie?'

They all stared at me, waiting. The door of the room they had me in was made of swirly glass that you can't see through. Blurry shapes passed backwards and forwards on the other side of it, like ghosts in another world. I nodded.

'Right. So you're saying that you did realise fires are dangerous.'

'I made a mistake. It's never happened like that before.'

'So you've started fires before?'

'No. I've never started an actual fire on purpose. My phone went weird and sent out hot beams. Just like I said in my journal.' I stopped. Six eyes stared at me. 'It was an accident. It's not how everyone makes it sound.'

'So you are aware then, Alfie, of how this sounds.'

Trapping me. With my own words.

'You can see that lighting a dangerous fire that gets out

of control makes people concerned about your own safety and that of others.'

'I didn't light it. It was an accident.' A tear rolled out of my eye. I didn't wipe it.

'And at Ash House. Did you have the same feelings about fire when you were there that day? Had you forgotten how dangerous it had been on the recreation field when that fire got out of control?'

The neck of my T-shirt was now in my mouth between each sentence I spoke. 'No, cos I didn't light a fire at Mr Clemm's. Why would I?'

'Why did you do it on the recreation field?'

'That was an accident. It was my phone. It got hot.'

'But it's something we all agree on, Alfie – that you started the fire on the recreation field. So to move forward, we need to find out why you did that.'

Round and round in circles. 'My phone did that. Not me.'

I read the suit woman's file upside down and saw *SELF-HARM RECOGNITION TRAINING* in capitals.

The suit woman sighed. All the woodwork here is painted cream, but they've used too much paint, and it's thick and wet-looking. It's upsetting to look at, and in that room, with everyone staring at me like they were so disappointed, it felt doubly terrible.

'So, Alfie, do you think that your actions on the rec field that day were a good idea?'

I squeezed the chair again and shook my head.

'Can you tell us why?'

My eyes settled on the thick, drippy paintwork. 'I didn't know what I had was burning hot, and it got out of control.'

'OK. Yet you did the same again at Ash House?'

'No! I didn't! Mr Clemm's machine probably started that fire. I said that already.'

They murmured to each other. I heard, *only for children with persistent conduct disorders*. I'd made a hole in my T-shirt with my teeth. Thoughts of Whizzy flew round and round in my head, but I felt empty and hollow. Telling them was the only thing I had left, so I took a deep breath and said, 'I found a creature that spews electricity. She got in my phone. It's all in my journal.'

Silence. Sideways looks went between them.

I pictured Whizzy looking at me with her trusting mirror eyes. I pictured her getting confused and agitated and her colour changing from white-gold to blood-red. Tears came, and sniffing and blinking them away didn't work. Two heavy ones leaked out and rolled down my cheeks.

'I understand that you moved from the city because your sister was being bullied and got very poorly, Alfie.

Do you want to talk about how the worry of that made you feel?'

My stomach clenched – they were going to ignore what I said, as though it was a silly made-up story or a lie! Anger boiled up from my chest.

'Alfie?'

'No,' I said, and kept my eyes down.

'OK, Alfie, we're going to leave it there for today because I think you've had enough. But I want you to carry on thinking about all the things we've talked about today in your own time. Is that OK?'

I nodded.

'Sometimes we do things without thinking about them much, without a clear reason. We can all do that. We don't always mean the things we do, but I want you to carry on thinking about the consequences of everything you did on both occasions, and we'll all get together again in a day or two for the next session.' The suit woman nodded at me while she spoke, then smiled and said, 'Time for your tea, I think. Hungry, Alfie?' Chairs scraped the floor as everyone stood.

I nodded, but I wasn't hungry. Not at all.

35

Not at Home

25th August

This place is stupid. Just when I find out that you can't be full-on scared or upset forever, someone comes along and ruins it. I'm not saying I was happy this afternoon, but I wasn't screwed up into a ball any more. I was doing normal things, like eating and playing pool.

Things we don't have: Any kind of water that hangs around, so no pond outside. No baths – only showers – no plugs in the sinks. No sharp things, so the knives are blunt, and there's no dartboard. You never have seconds of anything at dinner either, because if you leave your juice cup on the table, it'll have something floating in it when you get back. Food, if you're lucky.

But we do have an Astroturf pitch for football and

tennis and basketball courts. And there's a games room with a pool table, football table, table tennis and a Wii. That's where I've just been, until this happened.

There were three other boys around the pool table – Matt, Olly and Dev. They were all laughing and joking. Things seemed friendlier and I started to relax a bit, and suddenly the urge to let go and talk about everything got too strong. It all burst out of me. I started at the beginning, with the Cloaked Strider, the trespassing, and then Whizzy. The boys were silent. They were listening so perfectly, I thought they were rapt, so I carried on and spilt the whole story.

Olly winked at the others and grinned at me. 'Yeah, right.'

My face started burning. 'It's true.'

There was giggling. Sniggering. Then cackling and snorting.

'How big?' Matt asked, smirking. '*This* big and then *that* tiny and then *weeeeeee!* It's *ginormous* again!'

'An electrical *stringbean*!' Olly said, trying to sound like me. 'Freaky!'

Then he whooped and I stalked away from them and pretended to get interested in bouncing a table-tennis ball on the floor. It was awful.

A bit later, there was a game of pool and I tried my best

to forget all about it. I'd potted the blue, left the white lined up rubbish, tried for the green and missed. Olly potted his red and sent the white skittering down after it, and I laughed. That's all, but suddenly he's yanking my elbows behind my back, holding me face down on the table and hissing, 'What's so funny, freak?' in my ear.

His grip was *so* tight. Tears came into my eyes, but straight away Miss Jukes's voice filled the room – she took over from Miss Hughes when her shift ended. 'That's enough over there!'

She zipped across and Olly let me go. 'Perhaps a spell on the table football instead, Olly? Alfie, can you play Matt now?'

But I shook my head and raced out of there.

Near the dining room there's a quiet room full of books and board games. I felt like running and never stopping, but I picked up a book with a picture of a winged horse on the cover, then sat in the window and waited for my heart to stop banging.

I read the first page of the book, then heard footsteps in the corridor. It was Miss Jukes.

'Are you all right, Alfie?'

When I nodded, she did a kind of sighing smile and came into the room properly.

'That was your first skirmish. Are you going to come

back through and finish the game? Put it behind you?'

I shrugged.

'Remember, Alfie, this isn't a place for punishment. We're here to look after your well-being.'

She made it sound as if she's some kind of parent. But I'd BE a hell of a lot more WELL if I could just go home!

'Have a little think, if you like, but do come out soon. Always best to get back on with whatever you were doing after incidents.'

At home, I might be eating Mum's chilli jacket potatoes. I nodded, as if I was going to do what she said, then went to my room to change my sweaty T-shirt. The clean one made me think of home again because it didn't smell right, even though it's from home. It smelt of the drawer.

I couldn't go back out in the end. I switched off the light so they wouldn't know I was in here and I tried to go to sleep, but I couldn't. So now I'm just writing.

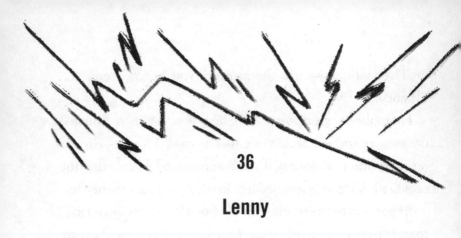

36

Lenny

At lunch today when we were let outside, I went and looked at the fence. It's massive when you get close. It's alarmed.

You'd never make it out of here.

There was no interrogation today, so I've been in the TV room. A new boy, Lenny, has been in there with me the whole time. I found him unscrewing the screws on a table.

'Are you sure you should be doing that?' I said. He didn't even look at me. 'Because—'

'Get stuffed.'

'Where d'you get the screwdriver? If they see you with that, they'll—'

'They won't see me,' he muttered. 'You tell them, and I'll end ya.'

He looked scared even while he was saying this. I picked up a car magazine and pretended to read it and he carried on, loosening all four legs just enough to make sure the table still looked normal. I felt kind of sorry for him.

'It gets better here, you know,' I said. Can't believe I said that; it isn't even true. 'Well, I mean, the first few days are the worst. You get used to it ...' Truer, this.

He looked at me with very sad eyes, like the saddest baby animal, and I left him alone, but later, at the dinner table, he sat next to me. He ate in total silence, then sort of followed me back to the empty TV room.

I tried to chat, but he wouldn't talk back and I couldn't even watch the programme because Lenny made noise in a big way. He dragged that screwdriver up and down the metal window fastenings, then leaped about re-screwing everything in the room that had a screw, as if he thought he was a proper workman. *Scratch. Rasp.*

Then he sat in the low window seat and scraped, as if the metal was his sculpture. The setting sun streamed in behind him. The outline of his hair looked like it had been painted with a highlighter pen. *Scrape. Screech.*

'Miss Jukes or someone will hear that and come in here,' I said.

He ignored me.

I like the TV room, and not just because of the TV – it always smells of warm furniture polish. It covers up the school smell and makes me feel like I'm somewhere near our old house in the city. If I close my eyes and breathe in, I can pretend none of this has happened.

But Lenny was ruining it.

I gave up and went to leave, but then Lenny suddenly spoke. 'Are you scared?'

'Scared of what?'

'Of what's next.'

I shrugged, and then he said, 'Why're you in here?'

I waited for a moment, in case it was a trick. The others might have got to him. Then I told him, bit by bit, watching his face carefully. His eyes grew wider and wider. He didn't laugh. There was shock on his face, but no sneering. He believed me.

'Whoa,' he said on a very long breath. 'That's amazing!'

I felt lighter instantly, as if Lenny had pulled a plug in my head. 'How about you?'

He fiddled with a bit of purple plastic from a broken pen top instead of answering.

'Haven't they told you?' I asked.

He swerved the question and said he wanted to know more about Ash House and Mr Clemm and the animals. I gave it to him, and felt better and better.

'And the big bird. Lysander. What happened to that?'

I gave him a sad smile. 'Nobody knows.'

'Probably flew out the window,' Lenny said. 'Glass breaks in a fire. He's probably free.'

Hadn't thought of that. Perhaps he was with Godrell. Perhaps they'd made friends. 'Hope he's all right, then. He only eats fruit, I think.'

'Plenty of berries about. Apples.'

I thought of the trees in Mr Clemm's garden. I thought of Lysander flying free, making a noise like a steam train. 'He's really old.'

'If he was in Nigeria, he'd be able to eat more. It's so hot there, you can grow any type of fruit, and when it rains, it's big, big drops, man, it's like standing in a waterfall. And they have lizards running up the walls all the time. Brilliant colours, like a rainbow. You should see them.'

Lenny's grandad is Nigerian. He talked easily now, mostly about Nigeria, where he plans to go when he's older. He's in here for thieving. Says his older brothers got him into it. He still collects things he finds lying about, but now he's stuck in here, he thinks it'll be mostly rubbers and rulers and Sharpie pens.

'So this bloke – Mr Clemm? He wasn't a weirdo after all.'

'No. I think he's just quiet. He didn't bother with anyone much, so people made things up about him. And he's very tall, so, you know – he looked really different.'

'People make up stuff about me and my brothers all the time. I know how he feels.'

'Me too.'

_10.00 p.m._

It's bedtime and we've been rounded up. Someone's kicking the wall outside my room, Miss Hughes is shouting, and the biggest, tallest care worker – Mr Danowski – is pulling someone down from a door frame.

This place is full of people. And full of anger and fear and frustration, and Whizzy's not even doing it.

And it's full of spit, too. They do it all the time, mostly without the staff even noticing. You can see it along the corridors and on the carpet in the games room: little globs of disgusting, bubbly spit.

I've written a letter to Sam telling him that things are OK, so that he won't feel too bad. Because I can kind of see how he must have felt now. About Whizzy. And the other stuff, but I'm not writing that down again.

37

Scraping Through

Just had another twenty million questions. I don't want to write about it.

You can see the door to the question room from the dining hall, and it was dinner-time when they let me out. When I sat down at a table, someone drew a square window in the air with their finger and put bars on it, then mimed '_prison_', pointed at me and nodded. They all started doing it. They all laughed.

At the end of dinner my food was untouched, but the boy carried on doing the mime all the way up the corridor to the games room. I don't know his name.

'You're going down, big-style. You'll never get out.'

I shook my head at him.

'Yeah, you are, cos you're a murderer.'

'I'm not.'

'You are. Murderer! Arsonist! Arse!'

Midnight

Something's just smashed outside my door and woken me up. Tried to snuggle back to sleep, but can't stop thinking, so might as well write it down, and my heart's racing.

They think my journal's just a load of made-up stories, not the truth about Whizzy and her electrical mangles. That's obvious.

Prison. Going Down. They say I'm only here until the proper court hearing, but after that, will I have to come back here or go somewhere else? The others made it sound like there was somewhere else. Somewhere worse.

Wish I could smash something. A plate. A chair. Or crack a mirror. The doors here can't easily be slammed because they're all slow-close fire doors, but it would be good to pick up a table and crash it into a wall.

I know why the others smash and shatter things. I know exactly why.

38

Visitors

2nd September, 5.10 p.m.

I felt sick when I realised the date: everyone at home went back to school today.

Miss Jukes has just knocked on my door and told me to wash my hands and face and change my T-shirt because I've got visitors. She wouldn't say who.

'A surprise for you, Alfie,' she said. 'Come to the visitors' room when you're ready.'

7.20 p.m.

I felt wobbly walking down to the visitors' room. I just had a funny feeling. Miss Jukes's face was soft and smiley, so it must be somebody good. But when I walked through the door and saw Mum's hair spilling on to her shoulders as she turned her head, I still couldn't believe it. A high little laugh came out of my mouth and Mum gasped, opening her arms.

'Alfie!'

And then I saw *Dad*!

Solid Dad. Not on a video – real.

They hugged me so tight it almost hurt. First Dad, then Mum, then both together, which doesn't really work if you need to breathe, but I didn't care.

'How's our Alfie, then?' Dad said, scooping my hands up into his big ones and blowing a tickly whistle down my fingers. He looked different, creased, like he hadn't been to bed. Last time I saw him in real life, before he went to Sweden, his face was fatter and he didn't look so tired. But his voice was the same deep Dad voice. And he's had a Swedish haircut!

'Who's mixing all the steel?' I asked him.

'Somebody else.'

'How's your tummy, love?' Mum asked. 'I've told them you suffer with your tummy when you're worried. Hope they've listened.'

'Dina,' Dad said, rolling his eyes. 'Alfie's storing up his farts to jet out of here in a couple of days, aren't you, Alf?'

I chuckled and went to stand behind him so I could

tunnel my fingers into his new hair.

'Can they even do African hair in Sweden?' I said. It looked quite good.

'They can and they have,' Dad said proudly.

I felt Miss Jukes watching us from her chair. 'Where's Lily?' I asked.

'She stayed behind with one of her school friends,' Mum said, smiling. 'We wanted to have you all to ourselves.'

'Was it on the news? Ash House …? Me?'

They didn't answer for a moment. Mum tried to keep smiling. Rain pattered against the window in little gusts of wind. Then Dad said, 'The incident was mentioned, but you weren't named, Alfie.'

I went to sit down again. 'But everyone'll know they think it was me. Everyone at school.'

'Alfie,' Mum said, taking hold of one of my hands, 'you're not to worry about any of that. We're working night and day to sort this out—'

Dad interrupted her. 'We're one hundred per cent here for you, Alfie.' He tapped the leg of his chair to make each word definite. 'We're *not* going to stop *fighting* until we've got you *home* where you belong—'

'Yes,' Mum said, jumping her chair over to mine completely and cuddling me. I let my whole weight rest against her.

'How's Lily? Is she still eating more and seeing friends?'

'She is,' Mum said, 'and it's miraculous, but we're not worried about Lily today, Alfie. We just want to look after you right now.'

'Lily rebooted!' Dad said, and boxed me gently in the ribs. He made it sound like something genius and amazing I'd done by myself. 'And, Alfie, I owe you an enormous apology,' he said, and my eyes flew open. 'I've spent the last two years so focused on Lily's trouble that you've slipped right through my fingers. I'll never let that happen again, and I'm so, so sorry.'

'So you believe me now? About Whizzy?'

'Lily's told us what she saw,' Dad said. 'Sorry, Alfie. I thought that journal was just your fabulous imagination. I had no idea those were real daily events.'

'I wish you'd told us right at the start, Alfie,' Mum said quietly.

'You wouldn't have believed me,' I said. 'And I had to keep Whizzy safe.'

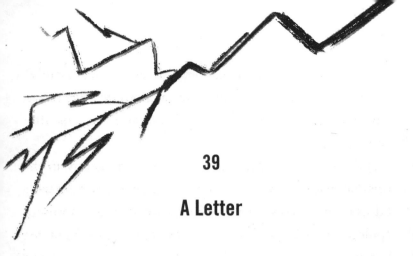

39

A Letter

<u>4th September</u>

I'm shaking so much I can hardly write. I've run all the way back up the corridor because of this letter! It's from Sam:

Hey Alfie,

Hope you're OK. I'm really, really sorry I left you on the rec that day when I could have backed you up. I keep thinking about it and wishing I'd just stayed and told Mr Lombard it wasn't your fault.

I didn't realise you never told anyone I was there. You plonker. But thanks. Seriously. I've spilt it all now. A bunch of scientists came to investigate the weather stuff in Folding Ford! Two women and a man. One of them stood with half their body in the rain and half completely dry.

Anyway, I told them about the fire and the weird stuff (Mum came with me) and they've sampled the ground and air around Ash House. They're going to prove you didn't do it. They'll find evidence of Whizzy. When she was in that box and trying to escape it, she must have sent disruptive magnetic and electrical disturbances over the village, and there will be traces left, so even if they don't believe me they'll see the truth when they log everything.

I told the police too. So you'll be out soon.

And remember our mega football game on the rec that day? I've found out that every brain has a magnetic field, so maybe that's how Whizzy made our game so amazing: magnetic interactions.

Sorry about what's happened to you. It could have happened to me. Everything before that was the most fun I've ever had!

Guess what else? My grandad spoke a word yesterday! He said YES. It came out funny, but it's a good sign.

Sam

PS: There's me, Mrs Gillespie, your mum & dad &

your sister all trying to get you out, so don't be sad!!!!!!!!!

   ; >)

   PPS: Also, I've googled electricity in animals *and the Oriental hornet converts sunlight into electrical energy. I'll show you when you come out. Or if you've got the internet there, just type in* ORIENTAL HORNET. *It's awesome.*

There was a colossal printout attached to the letter. Sam's looked up magnetic tunnels between Earth and the sun too, and wow. They happen about every eight minutes.

Miss Jukes let me read my letter in the quiet room. She'd opened it and read it first, in case anything was smuggled inside, I suppose.

'That seems great, Alfie, but we have to follow police evidence and if you were going home, I think we'd have heard, so don't get your hopes up too much.' She started to walk away, then turned to look back at me. 'Sounds like your friends have mustered up a little revolution for you. That's lovely, Alfie.'

She closed her mouth, but her lips quivered, as if they were full of things she couldn't say.

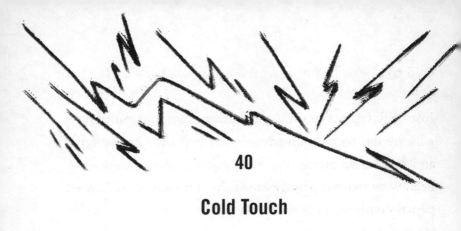

40

Cold Touch

<u>12th September</u>

More than a week's gone by and nothing's happened. Sam must have got it wrong, like Miss Jukes said.

Didn't eat breakfast just now. Couldn't. No saliva to eat with, and how can you eat without spit? This must be *exactly* how Lily felt. So I left early and came back to my room to look out of the window. I prefer to wait here.

The glass is wet with condensation and I'm making patterns in it. A solar system in the corner, then a whole tiny galaxy below it.

Just back from Art. Olly got on to me again. Don't know why he has to pick on me. He crashed over to my table and sat staring at me with a monster face, drumming his head with two fat paintbrushes. Then he held a sharpened pencil centimetres from my face, but he did it too slowly for the teacher to see.

'Why not?' he said, over and over, making no sense.

I moved to another table. Olly followed. I moved again and we made patterns around the room like that – chairs left at funny angles, people's heads moving to follow us – until the art teacher went to fetch Mr Badami, the PE teacher, for extra strength.

After that, Olly was unstoppable. Every type of paint, every colour, every texture. They only let him have one big sheet of paper, but he painted it like a mad French artist – only with more words, frantic, like a firework in a chemistry lab. Until he got too loud and Mr Badami terminated him.

Haven't been trained to do anything at all yet. This place has the wrong name.

NEW JOURNAL

13th September

They came for my notebook today. Miss Jukes came right into my room for it.

'All the pages, Alfie. We need to see what you've been writing about. But don't worry, you can carry on with a fresh book here. You can keep writing it out.'

'My laptop had everything, the whole record—'

'It's OK, Alfie – we know. Calm down. It's different this time.'

She looks like she's had a shock.

'What's different?'

'Other agencies have been investigating your case, Alfie.' She's looking at me in a way nobody ever looks at you in here: like she might believe me. 'It seems as if some new factors are coming to light, pet. And your journal is very important.'

She takes it from me delicately, like it might melt. Her eyes are watery after I hand it over. I want to tell her she's got blue liquid running on to her cheeks. Have they finally worked it all out? Am I going home?

<u>*15th September*</u>

Nothing's happening. Miss Jukes is avoiding me.

Waiting's worse than before she said anything. I hate this bed. And this desk. And this window, this grey sky. It should rain and pour and thunder. This is boring, tragic, gross nothingness.

Other agencies have been investigating your case.

So why don't they come? And who are they? What if they're not coming?

There's a buzzing in the air, like a low hum all the time that's making me even more twitchy, like my skin is full of ants.

There's been a strange sign today: ice. A good sign. Underneath one of the classrooms on stilts, all over some leaves. (There are always leaves under there, and woodlice live in them.) Almost didn't notice at first – the ice was so thin and delicate. Hardly there. It might shatter if you even breathed too close. I picked up a leaf and skated my finger along, and my heart raced when I saw how insanely thin it was, like the cleverest layer of the smoothest, coldest glass.

The weather's warm, so this can only mean one thing, but I hardly dare hope.

<u>16th September</u>

I'm shaking writing this. Whizzy is DEFINITELY HERE. In Maths just now, the plug on Mr Horvat's computer started smelling really hot and scorched so he switched it off and burned his finger. But the page projected on to the wall didn't switch off straight away. Instead, numbers and equations slowly dribbled on to the floor.

Then everything metal in the room heated up – door handles, chair legs, pencil tops, the staples holding our work-sheets together, those metal rods that hold the floor covering in place – and Olly and Matt started using some of the hot stuff as weapons.

Mr Horvat yelled, 'How are you doing this?' at Olly. 'I know it's you.'

Olly swore it wasn't, but Mr Horvat hauled him off to the quiet room anyway, and while he was gone, this mad humming started up in the walls. It was much louder than the other day – a proper electrical buzz, like the noise a fridge makes magnified by twenty.

Lenny and I looked at each other.

'It's your Whizzy, isn't it?' he whispered. He looked monumentally excited.

I had to frown my eyebrows like mad to get him to calm down without anyone noticing.

'Get me an intro to her!' he hissed.

I shook my head. 'It doesn't work like that. I can't control her.'

'Ah, please? This whole thing is *so* cool!'

But it wasn't as simple as that.

After lunch – where the cutlery was almost too hot to use – the humming got worse. It was in the ceiling as well as the walls. It thrummed through everything that had any kind of electrical wiring, and it got inside your head.

Even Lenny looked fed up with it. His feet were tapping with irritation.

'It can be awful as well as awesome when she's around,' I told him. 'I don't know which way this will go.'

41

Splinters

17th September

Today, the humming got SO BAD.

In Science, Olly just lost it. I mean, he went completely off his head – fingers in ears, head shaking, growling like a lion and kicking everything away from him brutally – chairs, people, books. Miss Hughes couldn't get close enough to control him.

'Right!' she yelled. 'Everyone outside IMMEDIATELY! This is now a games lesson and I'm going to get Mr Badami to take over.' She hustled us out of the door with one hand and pressed the other one flat against her forehead, like she needed to hold her brains in.

It was warm outside. Before Mr Badami even got there I'd dodged a dirty tackle – in an impossible move – without getting hurt, and scored an amazing goal. The wind started making a *whoo* noise like it does through doors and window cracks inside – but we were *outside*. That's when I knew for sure that Whizzy was really close now.

Suddenly, it was absolutely freezing. The puddles on the Astroturf turned to black ice and the other kids started smashing it to pieces. Ice sat glittering like broken glass everywhere. Boys' faces were full of *wow*.

More staff came outside and mostly stood there blinking in total astonishment, but I saw Miss Jukes grinning. There must have been hundreds of sharp pieces everywhere, but nobody even tried to clear it away, because there was more ice spreading across the ground right in front of everyone's eyes.

'Yeah, it's me – I'm doing ALL of this!' Olly screeched at Mr Horvat. 'I'm superhuman, me!'

The boys carried on trying to smash the ice, jumping and shrieking like mad demons, but every time they broke into the water beneath, the splashes they made froze in mid-air.

'To me!' Lenny yelled, and I looked down at the football by my feet – I'd forgotten it was there. I passed it to him and he tried for a goal, but it bounced off the post back to me, and I lobbed it *straight through* the back of the net, leaving a magnificent, barbarous hole! My excitement felt like a wave I could surf on. Every gasp of breath took me higher – I was almost flying.

Immediately, I wanted to do it again, but the weather landed down on us. The sky darkened and lowered. Thunder rolled. A huge cloud spilt its bloated guts and a curtain of cold rain fell on the main building, as if someone was pouring it from about fifty taps. The Astroturf was now like a skating rink, but it wasn't getting any wetter. This was focused rain. *Whizzy* rain.

The cloud wasn't finished. It bubbled like a boiling kettle. I've never seen a cloud do that before, and I'm never, ever going to forget it. The whole cloud was a dark, rippling circle, like a cauldron, and inside it different, lighter clouds churned. The noise on the rooftops was deafening.

Lenny snatched at my shoulder and screamed, 'Look at *that*!'

And there was Whizzy, filling the whole sky, and she wasn't a sunhorse any more – she was a dragon.

She flew across the sky in fiery ripples. She wasn't the creature I knew, made of light or electricity or both – she was fire now. Actual flames. There were crackling, hissing and steaming noises all around, but the loudest thing I could hear was my own banging heart. And then she stopped flying and just hovered with her head down low, almost to the treetops, hanging over us and obviously searching for something.

And she found me. Our eyes met and my heart raced more than ever. She was magnificent in this form, but so utterly devastating and different. Flames from her underside licked out. The smell of scorching tree mixed with waves of heat and the sound of screaming boys, and I found tears rolling down my cheeks.

After that, everything happened so fast, it was like the Mandeville Centre was the target of a storm attack. Whizzy reared up, and in a move that was more shocking than anything I'd seen before, she travelled backwards through the air like she was getting ready to take a run at something.

I ducked and covered my head. So did the other boys. Some were running back towards the building.

The lightning started without any warning at all. Brilliant white flashes, so close to us that everyone was stunned. Too stunned to even run. A blinding flash of forked lightning zigzagged from the ground, through Whizzy, up to the cloud, then back down near the perimeter fence. Thunder crashed immediately, like the actual air was splitting apart, and Whizzy shot up skywards like a rocket.

A grinding noise started behind the hill. The fence hummed, as if it was joining in. Then the fence was struck. We all watched as the whole thing lit up at once with a crash and a crunch, and a blueish haze drifted sideways.

Bits of lightning broke off the main fork. First one, then loads, like little sparks, and they dived down and spread along the fence. The smell of electrical burning was strong. The Mandeville Centre sent out a zillion reflections from all the windows, like a lethal firework display.

Then it stopped.

In the new silence, everyone realised at once. The fence was down. Everyone moved forward. We scattered like we were balls on a pool table and someone had broken us.

Thunder crashed. I ran forwards, sweating, hoping, and puffing like a steam train. Somewhere overhead a wire sizzled, and I thought about lightning strikes, but I didn't care.

Other boys ran. Soon, the whole pack of us surged through a blueish haze of smoke and the Astroturf filled with noise again. There was shoving, people falling down, the beginnings of a monster panic, but we crushed through. My head was bashed against someone else's. My ears rang. If there was an alarm, I didn't hear it.

Then all my strength came back and I raced up the hill-side away from the others, like a wolf. The sound of the chaos behind me was terrifying.

At the top of the hill I made for a little group of straggly trees whose spindly silhouettes I've often seen from my window. They looked like friends. They were the only things I liked about that place.

They were like the last trees on Earth. I wasn't going to stop at first. Didn't want to look behind in case the staff or the police were following, but … where was Whizzy? She'd busted me out of there – and not just me – but what now?

So I looked. The mass of boys had gone sideways instead of climbing uphill. They were heading for the woods at the other side of the main track, which was quite a good idea, really – if they made it. I could already hear sirens in the distance.

Then the sky changed. The storm cloud split, as if someone invisible was slicing it open. I saw a flash of silver, a darting, wriggly streak of blue light, and then a shape that stretched high into the sky, long and thin.

And then I ducked, because it looked like she was falling out of the sky straight at me. She'd torn the cloud behind her to shreds. In the last nanosecond I chickened out and crouched down with my hands over my head. She must have passed really close because I felt the air move next to my hands, almost as if she'd stroked me.

I opened my eyes. There was no Whizzy, but the storm had moved up the hill and was nearly on top of me, and by the time I realised that and had stood up to run, it was too late. The wind rushed straight at me, smelling like the inside of a cave, roaring in my ears, and down I went again with a slam, trying to blink away the grit that had blown into my eyes. An enormous flash arrived from nowhere and everywhere at once, leaving heat behind, very close, and I remembered too late – trees aren't the best things to head for in a thunderstorm. My lungs went tight. My cheeks were hot. Streams of stinky black smoke rose from somewhere near my feet and I didn't know which way to turn, but a second later, the smoke was drowned by a deluge of wet. I can't even call it rain, because it didn't fall from anywhere – it just appeared.

Spit gathered in my mouth like I might throw up and I wanted to scream, but there was no air to get a breath. Whizzy came back, and she was big. Frightening. And busy, so busy, doing that yanking thing again to the air itself. I hunkered as low as I could get. There was no way to tell if she knew what would happen to me if I got in the way of her work.

Then a tearing sound crept up close behind and I was snatched into the air – it felt like a massive Hoover was sucking me – and I stayed there. Up. Suddenly I was *in* the cloud.

Gasping, winded – the breath had been sucked out of me – but I was rising. The air looked solid but I rose through it. Higher. The cloud thinned and I could see the Mandeville Centre below me now: a bunch of floating lights, like candles on the sea.

I tried to move. My ribs still hurt, but I could stretch and turn. Riding, that's what I was doing. Riding the air. Every part of me was cold, but not wet any more. The wind was blowing me dry.

My eyes were getting used to the wind and I realised the silver shape that kept flashing below me, then above, wasn't going away. Whizzy? There were no more flames. If it was her, she circled me in deep spiralling overlapping arcs, and my heart hammered. So Whizzy *was* doing this. That's what all the yanking had been for. Was it safe? Just *how*? Probably physics, but it felt like magic.

The whole world was made of rushing and cold and tiredness. I closed my eyes. I could just ride. Let the air take me wherever. Whizzy was in charge.

When I woke up, the spiralling silver shape had disappeared. The sky was now steel grey, like one of Dad's batches. Water droplets on my sleeves shone like pale little jewels.

Rising columns of air, and layers. Loads of layers. You think the wind is all blowing in one direction but when you get up high, there are layers of it, some going this way, some going that way. Highways in the sky. Cold and clean.

If I looked down again, there'd be fields and houses and rivers and cities. But that would be completely brutally bloodcurdling at this height. Not seeing was dreamy. Comfy. The sky felt like the sea and I was learning how to feel the currents. They were like waves. I hit warm pockets every now and then, and cold patches that swirled over my face like evaporated ice.

Couldn't look down. Had to. Couldn't.

I did it. And there was Whizzy below me, stretched out so thin she was a pale beam, white with a gloss of gold, like a ray of sunshine a mile long.

Like a totally excellent flat escalator.

Sam once told me about the spookfish, which can see up and down at the same time. If that's a fact (and it is), then what might Whizzy be able to do with air currents? The thundercloud was long gone now, so it couldn't be the force from that … Was she doing what I'd once thought Mr Clemm's contraptions did – suction in front then spewing out behind? Had she made the air thick enough to ride? *Whatever*. She was doing it. Holding me up on a carpet of air.

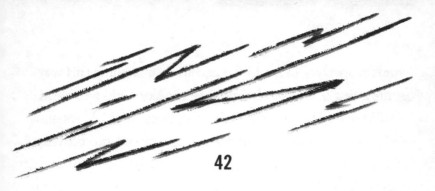

42

Rising

We climbed higher and things got rocky. Rough. A huge surge happened, like Whizzy was riding a wave, and my stomach fell into my bottom and lurched there, quivering. Wind flattened my lips and stung my eyes. At the other side, a wall of sparkling diamonds rose in front of us and all of my guts flipped over and over as we dived down, much too fast.

We skidded into the diamonds and I worked it out – they were just reflections of the sun shimmering in a cloud. We climbed again, even higher. Too high for me. Everything was going blurry and I felt floppy and weak. And now we were inside the cloud and I couldn't see much any more. Just flickering lights. That was all the sight I had left, but the sound of rushing air tore at my ears, and my face was drenched, and the rest of me was freezing. The air seemed too thin to breathe. My brain wouldn't think properly – I knew I needed more oxygen than I was getting, but at the same time, I felt too dreamy to care. It wasn't scary. Then it was. Then it wasn't.

There was time to think one thought about those rivers in the sky—

And then the lights went out.

Lily was sitting at the side of my bed. My own bed. I'm at home. Still don't know how. I reached out for her.

She jumped and yelped. 'Oh! I'll get Mum and Dad.'

My eyes are full of grit and my mouth's dry. Everything aches.

'Wait,' I said. 'What's happened? Where's everyone else?'

'You've been sleeping, Alfie. You made it all the way back from that custody centre – God knows how – and I found you in the hedge. You were missing for *ages*. The doctor came to check you and everything, and you still didn't wake up properly. You might be going to hospital – they haven't decided.'

There are things lined up on the bedside table that someone must have brought to tempt me awake. Toast. Lemonade. Grapes. Pieces of a broken-up chocolate bar.

She dived to the door then stopped and looked back at me as if she couldn't believe I was real. 'You sleep-talked. You said *great bustard*, over and over. I thought you were swearing at first, then I remembered Godrell.'

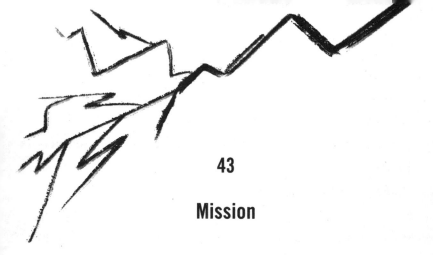

43

Mission

<u>*24th September*</u>

Someone very important came to see me today, and he apologised on behalf of the whole entire parish council! It was the new head of it. Mr Lombard has retired.

Mostly, getting an apology felt like a squirmy mass of cringey stuff, but the new man was nice. He tried to be quick but kept stopping and starting.

'Astonishing escalation of events,' he said, shaking his head (tufty eyebrows joining in). 'But all's well that ends ... The general rightness of things is ...' He cleared his throat. 'And all knots are as smooth as a dolphin's behind now, I hope.'

Lily was avoiding Mum – she was supposed to have cleared her stuff off the table hours ago – but I saw her listening at the top of the stairs and her shoulders were shaking with laughter.

Dad read out the final police report to all of us over pizza. It was some sort of reflecting device on Mr Clemm's machine that went bang. (That must have been the part that was supposed to attract Whizzy.) They think a fireball formed, and those can reach terrific temperatures. The top of his gadget blew off and landed half a mile away. The police have got it now, but some animals had mangled it, and that's why nobody found it.

Mum won't stop hugging me, and Dad keeps smiling and going mushy and repeating what a brainy idea it was to get everything down in that journal.

25th September

If you came to our village along the main road, you wouldn't notice Halfway Lane. You'd pass the shop and drive out of the village without even glancing up the little road on the left. But if you did take that left fork, and if you drove till you passed the last proper house in the village, you'd see the skeleton wall of Ash House. You'd see right inside to the rooms, like a doll's house with the door open.

I went back there today. Sam called for me.

He stood on my doorstep and held out his hand. I just blinked at him stupidly for a moment, and then I realised: he wanted to shake hands.

'Sorry,' he said, and it was awkward and odd, so I grinned and nodded, and that was awkward and odd too. But within seconds we were biking to Ash House without even telling each other that's where we'd go.

There was no sign of Whizzy.

'They say I dreamed that ride in the sky,' I said to him.

Sam looked all serious, and shot little worried glances at me like I might explode. 'Your mum told mine you were completely out of it for hours.'

I nodded.

'In the paper it said it took them three days to round up the boys they caught.'

'Yeah,' I said. 'Five boys are still loose, thanks to Whizzy.' I wonder if Olly's one of them. Or Lenny.

We looked at each other and burst out laughing.

'Hey, after they took you away, people on Usher's Place got electronic howling down their phone lines!'

'Ha!'

'Someone said she heated the whole landline system,' he said. 'Condensation on the wires started boiling and evaporating in full whizz-bang style. Maybe she was looking for you.'

When we got to Ash House, the green velvet chair from Mr Clemm's workroom was sitting in the garden. It still has the dent where he sat. The sides are grey with fallen ash, but it's all in one piece. Sam saw me looking at it and bit his lip.

I imagined the flames. The windows blowing out, the stairs collapsing. The black smoke, the curtains flaring.

Sam looked worried again, so I tried to smile.

'That's his chair, but I'm OK about it,' I said.

'It's too much.'

I shook my head. 'Not when you've been locked up for something you haven't even done.'

Sam let out a long whistling breath. 'OK.'

A little while later, he said, 'Wish I'd been braver sooner.'

I didn't know what to say.

<u>26th September</u>

This is the day I'll remember all my life, out of all the crazy days there've been.

Sam and I biked to Ash House again, and things started out ordinary. We've got used to the whole garden now. We know where the stone path crosses the boggy sunken patch and dips down, and how to avoid the trippy, sticking-up parts. We found the pond together. Dark green gloop glimmered on the surface like jelly, and it smelt of cabbages and wet soil. Scum floated around the edges today, but nothing moved, even though we kept still for ages.

'Still no spitting frogs,' Sam said.

'Unless they're lying low.'

We stood beneath the tree where the box used to be. No Whizzy. We started to laugh and joke and mess around just like the old days. Then we started to talk about where she came from, and how hot it might get in those space tunnels, and how she might have grown in the first place.

I had no idea but tried to sound like Mr Clemm. 'We'll probably never know. Nature solves problems in demented ways. Mr Clemm even told me he's got a butterfly in his greenhouse with *ears* on its *wings*!'

'So what?'

'It can listen for predators when it's flying,' I said.

'What's that got to do with surviving near the sun?'

'Nothing. It's just nature – it's amazing. Weird stuff's everywhere. Whizzy's just new.'

'To us,' Sam said.

That sank in quite quickly and made the back of my neck tingle.

'Probably helps if you're made of electricity, or light,' he said, 'or both.'

'Yeah,' I said. 'You're a hot burny thing to start with, so *whatever*, sun!'

We laughed *so* hard. I think we nearly forgot where we were, but then my phone rang. So did Sam's. Unlisted numbers.

'Hello?' we both said.

A crackling noise above our heads made us look up to see three perfect icicles hanging from Whizzy's tree, shining glassy and sharp in the sun.

Sam said, 'No way were they there before.'

I couldn't speak.

Then a speck of something bright appeared in the sky. A pinprick of light, a tiny flare, like a star on the move.

Moving towards us. And getting bigger.

Whizzy was right there in front of us in less than a second. Hovering only three steps away. Her golden electrical insides glowed and sparkled like the cleverest, most complicated plasma lamp in the universe. And every little movement she made sent a tiny ripple of electricity zinging out into the air. I felt it as a soft buzz on my skin. A sizzle down near our feet.

A faint, high-pitched whine came from our phones – both of them.

'Put them on speaker!' Sam said.

We did. The sound changed. Now it was like tiny, tiny

bells. Each little clink of sound evaporated into the air as fast as we heard it.

'She's singing!' I said.

Sam's eyes were round, shining, big. His whole body was still.

It felt like we listened for ages, holding our breath, but it was probably just minutes. If I could hear that sound again …

'Amazing, Whizzy,' I said, but something weird and shaky surged in my stomach at the same time. I felt like crying. 'How can we tell her to go?'

'What do you mean?' Sam said. 'Why?'

'She needs to go before someone comes. Before everyone in the world comes and ruins everything for her.'

But I think Whizzy knew.

It covered most of Ash House garden, and it was lightning, but not like any lightning ever in the history of the world. A vertical sheet of it stretched from the ground to the sky, as far up as I could see, a bright white wall, buzzing and crackling like it was alive.

Whizzy dived towards it, away from us, then turned back, all confused.

'Whizzy!' I cried, breaking away from Sam and racing towards the hissing wall of light. If Sam shouted after me, I didn't hear him.

The lightning wall renewed itself again and again, and this close, the noise was deafening. Sparks spat and popped, and underneath it all, there was a deep hum, like fifty electricity pylons.

Whizzy dipped and bucked towards me, as ripply and unsteady as she'd been that first night. My hands prickled. My teeth tingled and fizzed, but I smiled.

We gazed at each other.

'Whizzy,' I said. Her name came out of my mouth as a colour: bright orange particles, like light from a sparkler. I laughed, and the laugh rose like bubbles in a glass.

I stopped laughing. I said, 'You know you need to leave, don't you? Before someone else gets hurt? And before they hurt you.'

Her sunhorse head lifted and my heart felt wobbly. I tried to swallow the sadness, but it wouldn't go down.

'Find a magnetic tunnel, Whizzy. Be safe.'

Her head dipped. She turned a full circle one last time – golden, shimmering, beautiful – and I realised Sam was beside me.

Then she dived into the lightning and became a stream of light speeding towards the sky, almost the same colour as the lightning itself, but even brighter, weaving and billowing through it and away.

Like a huge dying firework, the lightning wall gave up. It collapsed, went *phut* and spilt over and into itself, fizzling out into nothing but a powdery charcoal trail.

When Sam spoke, his voice was all echoey and weird. 'She's gone.'

We stared at the mess of blackened earth where the weeds used to be. Whizzy had gone upwards, but it felt like I was falling in the opposite direction.

'Hope she finds the way,' I said to Sam, but I couldn't look at him, not with my wet eyes.

He didn't reply. When I gave him a quick sideways glance, he was nodding and biting his lip. After a while, he said, 'The tunnels are probably in a good phase.'

'Yeah,' I said. 'She's clever. She'll get back OK.'

But we didn't have long to think about it. We'd only been walking for a minute when they appeared: two men, one of them someone's dad from school, I think. Behind them came a couple of younger kids I've never met, then an older couple from Malusky's Corner.

Seconds after that, the whole village swarmed up Halfway Lane. OK, perhaps not absolutely the whole village, but most of it. They piled along like a pulsing wave, endless heaps of noisy, nosy people, all goggle-eyed, and all staring past me and Sam, looking for the weather display in Mr Clemm's garden.

44

Deliverance

27th September

And now I know what Whizzy learned while she was here. She learned that human people are soft things that have to be protected from heat. She learned that they can be transported easily: you lift them by juggling with the weather around them – a bit of warming, a lot of violence, make the wind strong enough to ride. Older people need longer to recover after they've been lifted and carried out of danger. If you can take them to very high ground, where hardly any other humans live, they'll stay safe and no one will bother them.

It happened after Sam went home. Mum came to find me in my room, where I've been happy and sad and crying and laughing about Whizzy since yesterday. She had a weird smile on her face – half frightened, half pleased – and I stopped stroking Julia, who was on my knee.

'What's up?'

'Something very strange,' she said. 'Very strange. And very good.'

'What?'

She gulped. 'It's Mr Clemm. He's turned up.'

'Alive?'

She nodded. I couldn't speak. My heart thudded and thudded and I thought I might throw up. *Turned up. Turned up.*

Julia was purring. I confused her by setting her down on the floor in the middle of a loud one, then asked, 'How?'

Mum shook her head and grinned like a zany clown. 'He's been halfway up a mountain in Scotland! Yeah. I know.' She shook her head again and again. 'He's been out of it, like you. Unconscious, but not in hospital. Badly knocked about, but not burned, and no smoke inhalation, nothing. He's very chesty, but that's because he got cold. He's been holed up in some out-barn with nothing but sheep and owls and goodness knows what. Nobody found him until a nosy hiker saw his coat flapping.'

I stared at her.

'We should be fuming, shouldn't we?' she said. 'All this trouble, all for nothing. All of it. But I can't feel anything but relief.'

'That's where she took him.' Up a mountain. I remembered that dark spot with Whizzy wrapped around it, disappearing over the horizon. I imagined Mr Clemm rising through the wind layers with dazzling, brilliant raindrops scattering behind them. Whizzy taking care, travelling further, keeping his soft human body safe. And then coming back across those hundreds of miles. For me.

'Where is he now?' I asked.

But I didn't hear what Mum replied because I'd leaped off my bed and I was off down the stairs and out into the garden, where Dad, talking to Sid next door at the garden gate, only just managed to stop me by pressing both hands flat against my chest.

_4.30 p.m._

Tomorrow, Dad says – that's when we can go and see Mr Clemm at Mrs Gillespie's house. 'Let the poor man settle in,' Mum said. 'He'll probably need to top up his nebuliser when he sees you, Alfie.'

Sam's coming too. Then we're going to the new skate park in Newton Moorby, because his grandad gets home the day after. Sam's voice sounded wobbly on the phone. Can't wait to get everything back to normal. He says even people we don't really know from the year above us at school want to see me. I'm an adventurer now; everyone wants a piece.

And Lily's heard a rumour: someone in the old people's bungalows has been leaving food out for a big strange bird.

'Don't get your hopes up though, Alfie,' she said. 'Everyone's yakking about your story. People mix things up.'

I've just shown Mum and Dad and Lily the spot where Whizzy disappeared. You can even see it from the road – part of Mr Clemm's hedge is scorched and blackened.

We talked about how lucky we are. We pretended we were joking, we covered it up in laughter, but we meant it. Lily and I looked at each other, one on either side of Mum and Dad.

On the way home, I rescued a biggish spider from a puddle and put it on the tarmac of Halfway Lane. It stretched all its legs out and skittered away, and that's when Lily saw it. She screamed her head off.

Acknowledgements

As Alfie would put it, the most colossal and ginormous thanks go to Salma Begum; this book would not exist if Salma hadn't discovered Alfie, or if Peter Kalu hadn't given him a chance back when Commonword launched their Children's Diversity Writing Prize.

Huge thanks go to my wonderful agent and miracle-worker, Abi Fellows; and to my fantastic editor and alchemist Lucy Mackay-Sim at Bloomsbury Children's; and everyone else on that brilliant team, especially Jessica Bellman, Sarah Baldwin, Beatrice Cross and Jade Westwood; and to Paddy Donnelly for the beautiful cover illustration.

More thanks go to the rest of The Good Literary Agency team, especially for Arzu Tahsin's developmental wizardry; and to the Northern Writers' Awards team, because winning that changed everything; to Fionn Kay-Lavelle for music and mentoring; to everyone at Atkinsons Coffee Roasters for making me so welcome in my second (and third) cafe homes; to King St. Studios for their artistic hub; to Lucy Nankivell and Judith Shaw for their eagle eyes; to Petur Højgaard Kristensen, Gail Rennie and Mike Robinson for ideas and critique beyond all sanity, and to all the other fabulous critters at CritiqueCircle.com, especially Harpalycus, Lola, Peter Martin, Lynn, Charlie Aylett and Jordan Elizabeth; to Sarah Dobbs for signposting and support; and to Simon at The Multimedia Shop, who saved me from computer Armageddon during final edits.

Special thanks to Andrew for all visible and invisible forms of support; to Peter & Dom for being yourselves and for all your funniest one-liners, and to Mum & Vernon for everything.